Charlotte was fascinated by the assortment of serpent skeletons and skins nestled under the old ranch house...

Gary and Elroy stared in awe at the grey/white bones that caught the sunshine. Suspended from the wooden scrap, they swayed and tinkled like the clay trappings of an innocent souvenir wind chime. Charlotte reached to touch the serpent's tooth, her hand somewhat slow and unsteady as she neared its sharpness.

"A serpent's tooth," thought Charlotte, who had been even more shaken by her encounter with this skeleton than with either of the two living reptiles she'd come across, "so small, so delicate, so seemingly devoid of life, yet filled with a venom that was every bit as lethal as ever it had been. Waiting, hidden and almost invisible, for an unsuspecting victim."

THE SERPENT'S TOOTH

A Texas Mystery

By

Kathy Borich

This book is a work of fiction. Any resemblance to actual events or persons, living or dead, is entirely coincidental.

"The Serpent's Tooth: A Texas Mystery," by Kathy Borich. ISBN 978-1-63868-033-8 (softcover); 978-1-63868-034-5 (ebook).

Published 2021 by Virtualbookworm.com Publishing Inc., P.O. Box 9949, College Station, TX 77842, US.

Dedicated to Gary, the wind beneath my wings.

Cast of Characters

CHARLOTTE CHOIRBY: Quirky English teacher who suspects foul play in Henry's death near the old ranch house that she and her family are renovating.

GARY CHOIRBY: Charlotte's professor husband, whose skeptical mind balances his wife's impetuous one. A naturally quiet scholar, when he speaks up Charlotte knows it's important.

BRANDY CHOIRBY: Charlotte and Gary's dreamy teenage daughter - quite focused when she needs to be - is the first to discover news of the "accidental death" of their neighbor.

DAMON CHOIRBY: Brandy's younger brother, full of youthful flippancy. He is insulted when queried on the Saturday cartoons schedule, but that knowledge helps solve a mysterious death.

HENRY SWEIGURT: A farm neighbor, notorious for squandering the family fortune on wine, women, and song, seems a victim of an accidental drowning ...or maybe not.

LUCILLE: Charlotte's feisty and shrewd ranch neighbor. A fountain of homespun wisdom on dewberry picking and avoiding diamondbacks in the process, she can talk without missing a beat, even with a Camel cigarette tucked under her upper lip.

CORVEL: Lucille's equally shrewd husband. Well hidden under his loose overalls and faded farm hat, his fine intellect remains hidden except for those few occasions when he decides to speak.

ELROY: A semi-retired carpenter, a whiz at water witching and killing diamondbacks with a single hammer-like blow.

TYRONE CARTWRIGHT: "Henry's pup," his half-black out-of-wedlock son. A fine man, blacksmith, and beekeeper, he rids Charlotte and Gary of a huge hive inside their ranch house walls.

CHRIS CAVECROFT: Owner of the patch of land next to Charlotte's, he shares a disputed fence line and pond with Henry, who was about to sue him over it before his demise. With Henry gone, that worry disappears.

FERNANDO MUNOZ: Perhaps the only person who actually did like Henry, his partner in some cattle they kept in nearby Taylor. Fernando is the first beside Charlotte to think Henry's death suspicious.

SHANNON CRATE: Charlotte's lanky former student, known for his outrageous persona and pranks, is now a prominent attorney in Houston. He and the "Emerson Branch" in Austin put the case together at last.

Contents

The Serpent's Tooth

CHAPTER 1
Rising Water

GARY PUT THE RECEIVER BACK ON ITS HOOK. He sat engulfed in the huge bed, an oversized pillow behind him, wooden writing board on his lap. Dazzling paisley sheets were lying in casual disarray at his feet. A nervous hand attempted to smooth the tousled hair of translucent gray that topped his shaggy brows.

"Charlotte," he called in a tone that said, please come help me deal with the world.

She opened the door to this academic retreat with reluctant compliance. Really those paisley sheets were a lovely bargain, she couldn't help but note, though they did lend an air of *Arabian Knights* to the bedroom/study. And her professor husband, with his fly-away hair and high Croatian cheekbones looked almost like some mythical Persian piloting a flying carpet; or maybe a lecherous Bedouin about to usher in his favorite harem girl.

"The horses are out. They're in Henry's pasture. Corvel said he herded Henry's stray calves back through the gate, and somehow the horses ran through. He couldn't get them back and had to close the gate. There isn't much of anything for them to eat back there, you know."

Charlotte remembered the bleached bones and skulls that dotted the pasture owned by Henry. And she couldn't forget the rusted pieces of barbed wire that seemed to grow from the neglected and weedy land.

"I'll go out right now and get them back."

"I'd go with you, honey, but..." He looked in frustration at the tidy piles of paper anchoring the disheveled sheets. Obtuse mathematical formulas were etched in decisive black felt tip on some, pages of esoteric prose on others, but even more ominous were the thick piles of blank pages on the wooden writing board.

"I'll take Brandy with me," Charlotte reassured him. "It will be relaxing for her after all those final exams."

Brandy retrieved the boots from the hall closet, sleek English riding leathers for her, and mud-coated western pig hide for Charlotte. With inner amusement, Charlotte made her way to the front door of their comfortable urban dwelling past first the antique writing table in the parlor, then into the living room with the old roll top, catching a glimpse of the huge wooden table in the dining room. Then she pictured Gary, engulfed by paisley sheets, floating on a sea of academic scribblings, with his back propped up by a pillow on their double sized bed. "Well, a writer writes where he wants, where he feels secure, in that personal nook that is found by instinct not logic," she reflected. Maybe the same contrary instinct, she thought, that makes horses leave a field of healthy Bermuda grass for an ill-tended pasture of weeds, barbed wire, and livestock skeletons.

The recent rains had created an emerald landscape quite unusual for Texas in June. The gently rolling slopes to the east of Balcones Fault defined the small oasis of black farmland just thirty miles from Austin. Not as thrilling as the rough beauty of the hill country to the west, this land offered the more serene beauty of a nourishing earth mother. The clay soil held precious water that just washed over the sheer rock cliffs to the west, held it so long and with such fierceness that a loose boot heel might be sucked off during a walk on spongy turf.

So, like a suddenly mature man who abruptly tires of giggling beauties and begins a quest for "a good wife," Gary and Charlotte had stopped traveling to the exotic hill country and began a systematic effort to secure land east of Austin. The forty-acre ranch, complete with ramshackle house, was the reward of two years of laborious searching. One horse expensively boarded at a stable had now become six who lived quite well off the fat of the land, country western music occasionally supplanted Vivaldi, and Charlotte now wondered if her training in classical violin would be a help or hindrance in learning to play the fiddle.

Brandy closed the ranch gate and hopped back in the Bronco just as the storm broke. A long narrow cloud, looking like a threatening charcoal snake above them, held its ground and refused to move on.

"Let's not even try to drive up to the house," Charlotte decided aloud. "In fact, I'm going to back the car closer to the asphalt. You know the water runs over the gravel road here right at the gate sometimes."

Brandy quickly relocked the gate, and the two climbed over it, resigning themselves to soaked clothes and drenched hair. Charlotte guided Brandy to the high grounds and was surprised to see puddles even on the hillside. The ground was really saturated; this rain would only run off the soaked landscape.

By the time they'd gathered halters, lead rope, and the all-important bribe of grain, the rain was pelting them in a soft but steady stream of huge drops. The front tank was spilling over to the green tree-lined valley, churning a narrow brown path down its center.

By now Charlotte and Brandy had given up dodging standing water, but they both kept alert eyes on the ground. Stories of snakes fleeing flooded holes to seek higher ground added tension to an already challenging chore.

"I see them, Mom." Brandy pointed to a slight rise about 200 yards the other side of the property line. The gate that once linked the cross fencing of Henry's 1000-acre ranch was now on the boundary of their forty acres and his last 100. It was a mute witness to more prosperous times. What was usually a pleasant dip of land under the gate became a moving swirl of muddy water, and

Brandy had to struggle to pull her boot from the sucking clay.

Charlotte looked for the best way back to the horses and saw only a few islands in a tangle of rushing rainwater. She and Brandy sludged their way to the stranded animals, first taking the depth of the many opaque rivulets that they had to ford.

They would only catch one horse, lead him out, and hope that the others would follow. This was their usual practice when catching the horses for a ride. Charlotte had made use of reinforcement theory, one of the few practical applications of her college psychology course, and rewarded the herd with grain in the corral at random intervals. Thus, she had surprised several seasoned horse trainers who were sure that five horses wouldn't follow one captured cohort into a corral. Sometimes academic training was unexpectedly relevant, she smiled.

It was easy to catch Abras, her stubborn gray gelding, even without the grain. The glistening horses were stoic structures almost glued to the muddy ground. At the sight of the grain bucket, however, they roused themselves and began a curious and greedy walk to Brandy and the aluminum pail. The slippery ground and circle of horses, each irritably vying for the grain, was suddenly an unforeseen and real danger.

"Dump the grain," Charlotte commanded. Brandy did so with quick compliance and backed away from flattened ears and warning kicks. That these menacing looks and behaviors were directed toward each other and not Brandy didn't lessen their potential harm.

The protective mother had rescued her offspring from harm, but at what expense? Now, as the remaining horses poked their muzzles into the yellow corn, oats, and sweet molasses on the ground, Charlotte wondered how much time this delay would cost them.

They had made it there with cautious determination, but some fifteen minutes of rain had bathed the saturated clay since then. Was the gateway a swollen river now instead of the earlier oozing puzzle? Charlotte led her gelding toward the gate, ignoring his resentment at being left out of the feast. Soon, the two youngsters were edged out by the three bossy mares, and they took hesitant steps toward Abras and the gate. Now Charlotte and Abras were approaching the gate with the two-year-old Shazaar and yearling Shazaara about 100 yards behind. The greedy mares had finished the soggy grain by now, but instead of following, they had resumed their earlier stations. Worse than that, the herd leader, Capzara, was calling to her filly, which now ran back to Mama, her delicate legs prancing high and mischievously in the mud.

"I'll get them," Brandy called, the worry in her voice mounting at the same rate as the flood tides. She went for her Silver Sun, the nineteen-year-old sprightly copper beauty that was the object of Brandy's devotion. Coaxing her forward, awkwardly pulling her head, and finally trying the other end with a resounding slap on her rear, Brandy succeeded in herding Silver Sun toward the gate.

Charlotte, never one to let a false sense of dignity obstruct whimsy, curiosity, or now necessity, began to nicker to the laggards. Soon Abras was encouraged and whinnied himself. His girlfriend, the maiden Silver Sun, answered and began to splash forward through the spongy earth and swirling water with renewed effort. The hesitant youngsters caught this enthusiasm and began again toward the gate, while Brandy yahooed and waved her hands to shove the last two mares forward. The smoky Meleoxon reluctantly slushed ahead, but a brave whack only rotted the stubborn Capzara to her ground.

They'd have to leave her then, and get the others out now, before the water rose any further. Charlotte and Abras tromped through the opening, going steadily until Charlotte stepped in a hole and went down to her knees. She might have lost her balance, but for her iron grip on Abras' lead. He dragged her forward a step or two and she was on high land.

The others ran through almost joyously with Brandy poised at the gate, closing it behind their tails.

Just as she was securing the chain, there was a blur of silver and a panicked neighing. Capzara thundered to a stop at the aluminum barricade. There was a risk in opening it, as Capzara might just as easily lead the others back through it as come through herself.

Brandy chanced it and opened the gate just enough to let the panicked mare through, but a few hesitant testing steps into the charging water and she balked. Brandy braved her touchy hindquarters with a well-timed slap, and finally, the troublesome beauty was through.

Brandy, whose dreamy teenage reveries sometimes kept her at routine chores forever; Brandy, who usually was the last one out of the house each school day, running to the car with shoes in hand or blouse askew, had closed and latched the gate, chosen safe footing through the water, and was suddenly behind Charlotte in shocking haste.

With a triumphant click, Charlotte released Abras, and the two humans watched the horses thunder through the rain to their favorite high ground, running with prancing legs and arched necks, with streaming manes and flagging tails, like carousel horses suddenly released from an evil spell by some repentant wizard.

The graveled road was now part of the brown stream overflowing the front tank, an opaque barrier some twenty feet wide between them and the parked Bronco. Bisecting it was the still locked gate, part of which was submerged in the muddy flow. For a moment, they felt trapped, unwilling to ford the current. Charlotte recalled front page pictures of helpless motorists stranded in the flash flooding that often-followed heavy rain here, snapshots of a stricken husband who had watched his wife being swept away by the powerful current. Sometimes horses, cows, and even cars were washed downstream in the engorged rivers.

From its mark on the orange gate, however, the water was only 8-10 inches deep, so Charlotte grabbed Brandy's hand and started to pick her way cautiously to the car. She chose her footing slowly, testing for sudden holes where sections of gravel might have washed away. The metal gate reached a welcome hand out halfway through the crossing. They climbed it quickly and leapt into the remaining water with relieved splashes. The Bronco was waiting patiently, its tires just touching the brown flow, like some venerable bather dipping its toes in water's edge while watching the younger generation frolic and splash in the greater depths.

With tacit efficiency, Charlotte and Brandy each crouched next to a front tire to turn the hubs to the lock positions. Even as they jumped into the car, the water had gained ground. Had they parked closer to the gate or been detained any longer, the Bronco might have been stuck, or possibly, washed into the ditch.

They would take the longer way home, avoiding the caliche roads and low crossings that were part of their usual scenic shortcut to the main highway. Charlotte stopped at the first stop sign, turned off the motor, and stepped onto the reassuring asphalt. With an awkward tug, she pulled off her boot to pour cupfuls of water onto the pavement. Brandy followed suit, and they both laughed. This had been the first relaxed moment since the storm had broken. But a glimpse at the rapidly overflowing stock ponds and drainage ditches reminded Charlotte that it was still raining. And they had a 35-mile ride back to Austin ahead of them.

It was a tedious trip, with the lashing rain obscuring visions and several patches of highway covered with water. One lightweight compact had washed into a ditch, its passengers waiting in the rain for the flashing lights of the highway patrol. Nearer to Austin, the storm was less intense, though, just a steady light rain that ran in civilized obedience into the waiting concrete drainage pipes.

So an incredulous Gary received their tales of flood and mayhem with raised eyebrows and cool skepticism. Only the evening news and reported road closings northeast of the city could corroborate their story. But the pooped pedant, eyes irritated and overused, was sound asleep by the 10 o'clock news and its brief coverage of the heavy rain outside of town.

***

Brandy slapped the paper onto the table next to Gary with such force that she nearly toppled his morning cup of coffee. She pointed with enthusiasm to the large picture and bold print beneath it on the front page: "Daring Flood Rescue." Pictured was a local volunteer fire fighter with a rope around his waist, moving toward an almost submerged car and the woman who was perched desperately on its roof. A second story was headlined, "Man Drowns Near Bridge Construction." Brandy read it aloud:

"A 59-year-old man drowned in his pickup yesterday as flood waters swept it from a temporary crossing at a bridge construction site in Williamson County. The victim, Henry Sweigurt, was apparently going to rescue some stranded cattle when he met with the tragedy. His body was found yesterday at 6:00 p.m. by a local rancher."

CHAPTER 2

The Old Ranch House

BACK ON LATE MARCH, even without the rain, Charlotte had had a problem herself with that bridge. She remembered it well:

She cast a grim look at her son Damon seated next to her. Charlotte should have known better. The red clay detour ramp was not meant for public access. The road was clearly marked, Bridge Out.

But she had made use of the local expedient, side-skirting the detour sign and taking the roller coaster mud ramp through the dry wash all of March without mishap, and she had become careless in that way reserved for vain outsiders and arrogant amateurs.

It didn't take much rain at all to slick the construction ramp, and it was only after she was part way down one side and felt the trailer behind her slip to the side that she noticed the slimy clay. Undaunted, with optimistic faith in American technology, Charlotte stepped out of the Bronco to turn the hub to four-wheel drive. Again the novice pride asserted itself as she felt in charge, maybe even a bit pleased to use the expensive technology usually not necessary in this snow-free climate.

However, the easy optimism was a thin veneer and quickly faded as attempts to back up met with horizontal rather than reverse momentum. An abandoned pickup on the other side of the ramp was more indication of the futility of the passage.

Then the dirty gray cloud above seemed to speak as the radio station warned of an oncoming storm cell reportedly dumping two to three inches of rain an hour. Already, the misty drizzle was changing to a more regular sprinkle.

Charlotte saw three choices. She had, unfortunately, already tested the most logical one and found that backing a trailer uphill on wet clay was not possible. Waiting was really no alternative at all, given the oncoming storm and their precarious position, not to mention the lumber behind in the open trailer. The third option, in that frenzied moment, seemed the only sane one. So with a courage born of necessity, she calmly stationed Damon as scout on the trailer, moved the gear to four-wheel low, and slowly began moving down the mud ramp.

The wet weather creek was dry now, but why had she never noticed how narrow and temporary the mud crossing was. However, she was beyond that hazard now and steadily moving up the steep ramp to the other side, only now realizing how close the abandoned pickup was to the red ribbon of a road. Charlotte steered the narrow Bronco to the very edge of it, remembering the eighteen inches that the trailer protruded on either side of it.

She had to ignore Damon's gasp and keep up her steady ascent until, miraculously, they had made it. For once, her teenage son's announcement was not exaggeration. The awed and strangely respectful voice was stripped of its usual flippancy and adolescent arrogance.

"We cleared that pickup by one inch, Mom. That was really close." Then, almost as an afterthought, an involuntary retreat to unaffected earnestness, "Good driving, Mom."

Elroy bent over his sawhorse and sliced through the wood. His agile frame and tireless effort belied the label senior citizen or semi-retired. A nod of his head and a shy smile acknowledged their presence.

"I think we're in for some rain," Charlotte announced. "I guess we'd better stack this lumber inside. I almost didn't get here with it," she added breathlessly.

Elroy listened with quiet amusement to Charlotte's narrative of her narrow escape from the dry creek. Damon, now composed, resumed his detached demeanor, and punctuated the adventure with wry remarks cloaked in scientific terms.

"The weight of the trailer really was a stabilizing force," he lectured. "The incline of the ramp was actually very gradual and calculated to afford street traffic as well as road crews."

The three had formed a kind of human conveyor belt and hoisted the 1 x6's through the sagging window frame in a steady flow. Charlotte was posted inside, where she received and stacked the still aromatic wood in neat piles in the one vacant room,

"Ouch!" Damon's energetic delivery of the lumber was getting a bit too exuberant. Charlotte instinctively lifted her hand to her mouth, and then removed the offending splinter.

"Slow down some, fellows," she reproached. "I'm getting behind, and my hands are beginning to feel like pin cushions."

The clap of thunder that immediately followed at first seemed to lead a stamp of authority to Charlotte's request. The ground even shook as in deference to her wishes. But its true warning was clear enough, and Charlotte soon found herself having to ignore the wooden needles as she hurried to stack the last rush of now rain-dotted timber.

Damon and Elroy stamped inside just as the big drops began. Elroy discarded the plastic wrapper and placed an unlit cigar in his mouth. He chewed it with philosophical absorption, gazing out toward the back pasture.

"Them ain't your calves out yonder?" he asked, nodding toward to rain the rain-soaked field.

"No." Charlotte strained to see the five black and white forms. "How long have they been there?"

"Last three or four days," Leroy acknowledged. "I didn't think y'all had any beef stock."

***

Damon and his school friend ran with the gaudy kite, letting the late March winds play throw and toss with them. The month was living up to its name, and the dry gusts now carried pollen that dusted cars and porches with army green.

Tommy sneezed. That was enough to upset his aeronautics, and the orange and red kite nose-dived into the earth. He looked at it petulantly and then turned his resentment toward the old ranch house that had silently observed his defeat.

"That's the ugliest house I ever did see." Tommy told Damon.

Charlotte smiled and considered the judgment. Well, yes, she guessed some might think it ugly. "A fixed upper," the real estate agent had called it. The seventy-five-year-old boards were gray with age, rough and gnarled with the years of blistering sun and the buffeting of blowing sod. One drooping side sadly donned the pale remnants of anemic yellow paint in the almost pathetic way an aged coquette still wears a gaudy brooch or reddens her lips. The three doors were covered with rusting corrugated metal, a belated attempt to keep curious cow away from the hay stored inside. That the barricade had been erected too late was testified to by the mauled and soggy hay intermixed with enough manure to fertilize three backyard gardens. An overriding odor of ammonia offset the would-be sweet smell of the unspoiled hay.

"Yeah, they had a good time of it. Was in there a week before Corvel knowed they'd gotten in," Lucille chimed in, apparently reading Charlotte's thoughts. Then, in an attempt to be the conscientious farm tenant, "Why, that hay in 'ere's no good, anyway."

"Just weedy Johnston grass past two years old." She lit a cigarette from the ignited butt in her hand, pausing in talk just long enough to tuck the new

Camel under her upper side lip. It hung limp and casual, like the fag of a cheap hood in some Bogart movie, only Lucille did it with more ease, expertise, and yes, even more class, than any playacting Hollywood actor could. The fascinating thing was how it moved as she talked, hanging there somehow like a stubborn baby tooth that refused to let go its last stringy hold.

"That lady didn't know nothin' about farming," Lucille continued, letting loose this greatest of indictments against the previous owner. The Camel flopped gently as she chuckled scornfully. "Only out here some three or four times a year, and then jest to pick them grapes--" she nodded toward the wild mustang grape vines hanging luxuriantly on the barbed wire fencing and covering the low thicket with green quilting. "Crazy about honey, too. Jest loved them bees."

Charlotte glanced toward the east side of the house. A low-pitched buzzing only hinted at the mammoth hives honeycombed throughout two sides of the L-shaped structure. The warped board and batten facade created the perfect creviced entry to a secure home for the honeybees; the wild clover was there in the field for the asking, and no one had questioned the bee's stewardship of the ranch house in at least twenty-five years. That would have to change. Charlotte made a mental note of it.

"Didn't they scare her? Wasn't she ever stung?"

"Why, I don't know," replied Lucille. "but she kep' bees in her backyard at home, too. Used honey for everything. Something against sugar. You know the type. One of them natural livers. Probably never let a good steak in her life, probably a dim vegitar'n, too."

"Yes, I remember when I made her tea, when we were closing the sale. She asked for honey then, but I didn't have any. From what I've read, it isn't really better for you than sugar..."

Lucille's weathered face was puzzled, her shrewd eyes squinted. She was certainly not interested in Charlotte's review of the honey-sugar controversy, or for that matter health foods or healthy living in general.

"Ya' know, for a vegitar'n," (Lucille's supposition had now become fact), "she could sure shoot a sow all right."

"What?" queried Charlotte, finished rambling on about sugar and honey, and now on to the mixed blessings of diet colas.

"That sow o' of Henry Sweigurt's. Killed it right here with a '22. Corvel saw her do it. But she was in her rights, ya' know. 0ld Henry's sow kep' on comin' over here and even charged her two kids--they can be vicious sometimes. She told him about it, but he wouldn't pen it up and it kep' comin' over. Poor hog. How could it know Henry didn't own this place no more. Kind a served Henry right, though. He's a terror for letting his stock wander,"

"Were those his cattle that got into the wheat field last month?" Charlotte wondered aloud, vaguely remembering Corvel muttering about Henry's cattle breaking down the fence and wallowing in the tender grain.

"Yep, it was. Don't wonder they get out. Not much for 'em to eat at his place."

Then they heard the low rumble of a perfectly tuned mechanical dinosaur, and Lucille, turning her head to the sound, waved to the overalled figure seated in the towering combine. "Well, Corvel's done with your wheat field for today. Now I've got to do some combining in Structure."

Deftly stomping out her Camel, Lucille strided over to the awesome machine, and with surpassing agility ascended to the air-conditioned cab. Her husband moved to the side, and Lucille maneuvered the 52-thousand-dollar giant with easy authority, looking perhaps more up to the job than her spouse.

CHAPTER 3

Nature's Bounty

CHARLOTTE WALKED TOWARD THE BACK pond or stock tank as they called it here in central Texas. What a utilitarian name for such a whimsical little lake. Each time she saw it on one of her weekly visits, it was different--angry and muddy after a storm, only to turn clear and innocently blue days later, like a cherubic child after a vanished fit of temper. One time in winter she had counted fourteen wild ducks floating there, then at her approach, seen them take off effortlessly at forty-five-degree angles, as if some magician pulled them up on hidden wires. This May day it mocked her; the frogs leapt into the water with insulted croaks and noisy splashes that never failed to make her start. A lazy turtle jumped from his rock to the safety of underwater, suddenly poking his head, snake like, out on top again, a gentle reproach for this disturbance. Only the skating water bugs and buzzing gnats ignored her intrusion.

A velvet black butterfly arabesqued past, beckoning her to the enchanted crazy quilt of wild flower prairie above. She followed obediently, as ever, enchanted by the delicate beauty that could exist in this often-harsh land. A few crested blue bonnets bowed imperiously in the breeze, complacent to be the state flower and grace any number of clichéd paintings, postcards, and photographs. Charlotte tolerated their presence, but her natural affection went to the lesser known more humble varieties. Blushing buttercups dotted the landscape, and crimson Indian paintbrushes reached for the blue and white palette of clear sky and clouds. Shy violet blossoms hid beneath grassy tufts while peach colored succulents lifted curious heads above the shaggy turf. Even the plain dried grasses and weeds held a natural and casual beauty. An especially inviting clump waved from a nearby gate. She pushed it aside to uncover the straw bouquet.

Tck-a-tck-e-tck-a-tck-

Instinct preceded thought, and Charlotte stepped back before the thought, "snake" was consciously registered. She saw it now, a brown and yellow rope parting the grass as it moved. She had nearly stepped on it. The swinging gate must have startled the diamondback, as it was now moving away from it and towards Charlotte. Strangely, she was somewhat grateful when it stopped, coiled itself, and began to rattle a warning to her.

How easily it blended into the black/brown soil and straw-colored grass. It was a strain to keep it spotted.

"Gary, there's a rattlesnake back here."

Her spouse was there now, but his plan was not particularly comforting.

"You stay here and watch it, while I get something to kill it with. Don't let it get away."

For some reason, that last remark didn't sound at all ridiculous. Charlotte was buoyed by her knowledge of serpentine habits, carefully based in an almost voyeur fascination that spurred hours of pouring over *National Geographic Illustrated Reptile Encyclopedias,* and other written sources. She'd read every *Reader's Digest* account of real-life encounters with snakes, and studied the labels at the reptile house with a thoroughness that tried the patience of her children when she took them to the zoo. Just recently, she had been fascinated at the Taylor Rattlesnake Roundup, featuring timed sacking contests between two-men teams armed only with a burlap bag and metal device almost like a pronged golf club.

A coiled snake, she repeated like a mental catechism, can only strike one-third the length of its body. Why, Charlotte was at least ten feet away by now, and the snake was between three and four feet. So when her quarry seemed to be losing interest, Charlotte moved a step or two closer, rewarded by his renewed rattling and her cautious sense of pride.

Only a naive high school English teacher from Chicago, where snakes were of the human variety, would be teasing a four-foot coiled Western Diamondback and actually enjoy it.

"This was all I could find." Gary was rather breathless, as he returned carrying an eight-inch landscape timber gleaned from the barn's new mud deck.

Now a real Texan would have gone to his pickup to retrieve a well oiled 12 gauge and dispatched with the critter in no time. The old timers would have brought a sturdy garden hoe, and some daring good of boys would have faced mankind's tempter armed with only a stout tree limb.

But her Gary, the self-made scholar, the professor of statistics who learned his early arithmetic on Chicago's south side, was more experienced fighting youthful street gangs or more recently, analysis of variance coefficients, than he was versed in rattlesnake warfare.

"Don't get too close! " Charlotte, the snake seductress, was now a worried wife.

In due deference to her concern, Gary loosened his grip on the cumbersome timber and walked his hands back nearly to its end.

The dull thud of the timber was followed by a cry of pain.

"My thumb," Gary moaned as he looked at the about-faced joint, "I've broken my damned thumb."

Meanwhile, the affronted reptile crawled slowly away from this human circus.

***

"And what is your problem?" The white-coated emergency room nurse bent over the seated foreign looking man.

"My tongue hurts," he whined, and proceeded to display the offending appendage like an irritated child.

The figure in white assumed a most serious expression and examined it carefully.

The admittance clerk poised over the computer as she looked vacantly at the shabby man in front of Charlotte. "And when was your last visit here?"

"Last Wednesday," he replied, and simultaneously the computer spewed forth his record, a detailed account as long as some government pamphlets, and as interesting.

"My eye still been bothering me," he volunteered. "I think I needs more of that pain medicine."

The clerk's dubious stare did not intimidate this regular customer. He waited expectantly, with an air of accustomed confidence.

"Be seated over there," she finally returned, rolling her eyes after he moved to the right.

Obviously Sunday morning was their slow time, and various patients timed emergency medical needs accordingly.

"But you should have finished the medicine even though you felt better." The nurse's words seemed a foreign language to her puzzled listener.

"I was all right last week, though. Its only today that my throat started hurting again."

A Job-like mask settled on the nurse's countenance.

"No, this is our first visit," Charlotte told the attendant, who seemed a bit surprised by a new customer on a Sunday morning. Charlotte looked anxiously at Gary, sitting on the bench in silent discomfort. A quiet man, he was almost mute in the face of physical pain, and his reaction toward officious bureaucrats was a rebellious refusal to respond to inane questions.

The nurse approached him with her Sunday morning air of patronizing patience. “And what is your problem?” she asked in brisk cheerfulness. He held up his dislocated thumb.

But she needed a verbal comment, some words to record on her clipboard duty roster.

The same mute reply and again the repeated brisk question.

“I’ve dislocated my thumb!” Gary finally informed her, somehow conveying his disgust that he, the patient, should have to make his own diagnosis.

“Oh,” she replied, somewhat chagrined. “And how did you dislocate it?”

“Killing a rattlesnake,” was the succinct retort.

“And did you kill the rattlesnake with your thumb?” she asked in all seriousness.

Gary cupped his good hand over his massive Slavic forehead, looked at the tiled floor, and slowly turned his head from side to side, a motion that voiced more contempt than any vulgar expletive he might have been thinking.

“You know,” the beleaguered nurse confided in Charlotte, as she watched Gary disappear into the treatment room, “I didn’t know what to say when your husband showed me his hand. A lot of our patients are just naturally deformed.”

CHAPTER 4
Dewberries

"YOU'LL NEED THESE." Lucille extracted a pair of oversized hunting boots from Corvel's closet. They were thick brown leather, adorned with scuffs and various colors of dried clay, made with deliberate scorn to style, and looked, Charlotte thought, perfectly horrible.

She stuffed her leg into the boot and found that it reached to just below her knee. Her denim jeans were manipulated inside and helped hold the cowhide contraptions on.

"Now we'll get you a good stout broomstick!" Lucille seemed to be enjoying herself, almost like a veteran knight arming his squire for a first battle. She rummaged with noisy abandon in the utility room. "This 'un 'ill do fine," she beamed, and handed Charlotte a weathered cylinder of wood about four feet in length. It was obvious that some period of time had passed since the wooden staff had been united in service with broom bristles.

"Make sure an dab yourself good with that kerosene." Charlotte complied with a certain reluctance, wondering if she might be setting herself up as a possible victim of spontaneous combustion out in the brutal sun. "Get yourself real good at your boot tops and waist." Lucille had noticed the lack of enthusiasm in Charlotte's anointment. "Them chiggers just love to get in where it binds. And with all this rain, they'll be fierce in your dewberry patch."

Charlotte relinquished any remaining hygienic fastidiousness, and fairly bathed herself in the odious liquid. "That's more like it," Lucille chuckled. "Now bring your bucket and let's go."

"You really think we need all this equipment just to pick dewberries?" Charlotte queried once in the pickup.

"Why no, if you want to be gathering snakes and chiggers along with the berries." Lucille laughed at her little joke, but Charlotte merely smiled politely, lost in wistful reminiscence of the ease of produce gathering at her local Safeway.

"These boots really do seem quite protective," Charlotte ventured with attempted enthusiasm. She tapped the brown leather in much the same way the inexperienced car buyer kicks the tires.

"Why, Corvel wouldn't go huntin' without 'em. A snake 'd have some time getting through them, though I've heard of some could bite right through them regular Sunday kinds. It's the extra length that helps, too," she continued. "You're safe clear up to knees, at least."

Charlotte tried to feel comforted by this somewhat limited testimonial. "By the way, Lucille..." Charlotte was eager to turn the conversation away from fanged serpents for a time, at least. "You were saying that Henry was wearing his best boots when they found him last week."

"Sure enough. It didn't make too much sense to me. Why. Henry never wore his custom boots when he was workin', or tryin' to look like he was at any rate." She winked at this allusion to Henry's well-known aversion toward physical labor. "Used to brag on them boots. Had 'em custom made in Houston and paid a good dollar for 'em, too. Alligator they was, though they didn't look any better 'n Corvel's Tony Lamas, which I bought for him last Christmas."

"Wasn't he supposed to be going to tend to his cattle or something?" Charlotte asked.

"Leastways that's what Fernando thought," Lucille answered.

They were at the drive now, and Charlotte jumped from the truck to open the gate, walking with an ungainly stride in the monster boots.

Lucille parked the truck in the shade of a low-slung mesquite tree, and was walking briskly toward the dewberry patch.

She was already at work when Charlotte arrived. "First," Lucille began, "you want to poke around real good with your stick." She made good her word with a vigorous beating of the dewberry bush and the spongy soil beneath it. "And look for holes. Don't bother with bushes if they've holes around 'em."

"I know," Charlotte hastened to reply, hoping to cut off the inevitable reference to lurking vipers. She was already pounding her victim dewberry bush with commendable passion and was almost disappointed to see no slithering beasts retreat from this assault. Next, she crouched awkwardly and began to harvest the violet jewels, occasionally testing their ripeness by popping one in her mouth.

But if Charlotte and Lucille were armed for combat to pick this sweet harvest, so were the bushes. Delicate thorns dotted the tangle of vines, extracting a price for each berry picked. With the unrelenting sun above, the threat of slithering vermin below, and the regular clawing of the protective vines at work level, there was kind of clipped conversation with long gaps, the kind of talk that usually accompanies hard physical labor.

"But why would Henry have to drive to get to his cattle, Lucille? I thought that all he had was this last 100 acres." She gestured toward the adjoining property, the fence line where refuge cattle had escaped from Henry's poor pasture into hers with regularity.

"You're right there. But he leased some land near Taylor. He had about 50 head there."

"So he was going there, to Taylor, when he was washed away." Charlotte thought about this as she put a battle-scarred finger to her mouth. The same bridge, she thought, where she had nearly been stuck. "But he was wearing his custom alligator boots," she murmured aloud.

"Yup." Lucille had found a particularly promising bush and was racking it with concentrated energy. Idle conversation about their deceased neighbor did not particularly interest her now. "Durn, these are big. I'll fill up my bucket in five minutes here," she chortled. "Come on down here, Charlotte. Must be because of the runoff, all that May dirt that washes through here."

Indeed, these berries were giant-sized, luscious velvety gems whose quilted texture reflected the sun like so many rubies. Thoughts of Henry and his alligator boots easily gave way to the pleasure of reaping this bountiful harvest. It is a well-earned reward for the farmer to reap the crop he has sown, weeded, fertilized, and protected diligently from marauding pests and blight. But a wild harvest is something else entirely. It is a return to the Garden of Eden innocence and the unearned bounty of benevolent Nature, or perhaps for the more skeptical, a vestige of the greed in human nature that caused the subsequent fall from grace. But Charlotte and certainly not Lucille did not ponder the philosophical or religious uncertainties that caused this magic; they merely fell under its spell and abandoned themselves to the unrivaled delight of reaping the wild bounty.

CHAPTER 5

Good Fences Make Good Neighbors

"THAT'LL BE $38.50, PRAISE THE LORD." Charlotte smiled somewhat uncomfortably and wrote the check. Her glance went from the bearded clerk to the young woman filing receipts behind the counter. The cotton print she wore was plain in the extreme, and it was more than the lack of makeup that robbed her face of youth or beauty, or even pleasantness. She had a drawn look around her lusterless eyes and a thin set mouth. Suddenly Charlotte felt her own jeans and T-shirt, and yes, even her smile, were out of place here, viewed reproachfully from those dull eyes. Here, apparently joy and happiness were as taboo as women in jeans with short hair.

The clerk of Metro Metal Supply approved her check, if not her dress and demeanor, and handed her the receipt. "Brother John will get the wire for you," he said almost pleasantly. Profits for the Lord, Charlotte thought, were certainly acceptable. And they always had a hope, she mused, of making converts of their customers. The office walls were covered with signs, most hand-made and more concerned with fervor than spelling or grammar. There was one very graphic one outlining the path of righteousness as well as the path toward sin. Their prices were the best in town, though, so Charlotte was willing to put up with this evangelical enthusiasm, this dogma of disapproval in small doses. She picked up a religious leaflet on her way out and met the eyes of the young woman behind the counter as she did so. What did she see in them--tacit approval for a possible convert, or just for a brief flicker, was the mask dropped, and did Charlotte actually see a wistful longing?

Charlotte always took a religious pamphlet when she left Metro Metal Supply. She attributed it to idle or even academic curiosity like an anthropologist examining a relic, the key to a completely foreign culture and its values. Or was she childlike, trying to wipe out the rebuff in those cold stares from behind the corner. She drove through the gate of the hodgepodge fence made to display each sort of metal barrier carried by the company and felt a great sense of relief, such as one feels at the end of a particularly long and tedious sermon. The open expanse of highway was exhilarating, and she edged the Bronco just over the speed limit. Or maybe, she thought with a twinkle, maybe she did it just out of mischief.

Chris Cavecross, her ranch neighbor to the south, was ready and waiting when she arrived. He raised Brangus, a breed of beef cattle combining the meat-producing Black Angus with the easy keeping Brahmas. The fence that separated them from Charlotte and Gary's Arabians was in bad shape, and Charlotte had negotiated the repairs--she would purchase the supplies and Chris would do the mending.

"I hope I'm not late," she greeted Chris, anxious to maintain his good will.

"Naw," he assured and shifted the lump of tobacco in his underlip. "I was just walking off this back fence line. I'll be stringing a new line back there. It's a good forty feet short of the property line the way it stands, and that tank over yonder..." He pointed to what Charlotte had always thought was Henry's stock pond. "That tank--" Chris paused to spit discreetly onto the ground, "–is really on my land."

"That will be a help. Then you won't have to come every day to water your cattle."

Chris, who owned some thirty-five acres, was in the unfortunate situation of having no stock tank on his property, and since he lived some eight miles away, had to make a daisy trip to fill a metal container with water. And the water was not easily gotten. During wet weather his cistern was full, so he would pump from that, but in the dry summer months he had to bring a large water tank in the back of his pickup and fill from there.

"Too bad about Henry," Chris said, his eyes on the back fence line, "though I don't mind telling you, it'll be a lot easier for me now because he's gone."

"Oh, you mean no more cattle escaping onto your pasture," Charlotte ventured.

"Oh, that," he smiled, "that wasn't the problem. No, Henry was about to sue me over that strip of land I just told you about. But it wasn't really the land, it was the water, and pure orneriness on his part." He here paused sharply, punctuating this last statement with a thin line of brown spittle directed at the cedar fence post. "Something called adverse possession. If he could prove that he'd used and worked that land for over ten years, he had a good chance in claiming it legally. If I would have changed that fence over when I bought this place six years ago, he couldn't have done it, but between my work in Austin at the bank, the house in Elgin, and these thirty-five acres, I didn't have much time to change out a perfectly good fence. Plus, I didn't even know about the property line being off until Henry told me last winter."

Charlotte was trying to lift the coiled barbed wire out of the trailer, but she could not get a good hold without the metal teeth biting into her skin. "How did he happen to tell you?" she managed between various unsuccessful handholds.

"Let me get that," Chris smiled. "It helps if you wear gloves." He had the wire coiled over his shoulder and had just stepped down from the trailer, and then he paused to look at her, as if the thought had just occurred to him. "You know, I don't think he'd've mentioned it at all, except he thought I already knew. I was mending the fence--after his runaway calves as usual--and he saw me back there with posts and wire. 'You're not gonna change that fence, now are you boy?' he said. Then he went on about how he'd been in the cattle business for forty years and how this whole section of land used to belong to him or his family. 'The papers might say it's yours, but 99 percent of the law is possession, that's right, possession. And me and my cattle've been possessing this here land since you was in diapers."

Charlotte tried not to stare, but was both repelled and awed by this latest display of liquid oral propulsion, the amber stream arcing at least eight feet, she was sure. Chris was reliving the incident now, and seemed completely unaware of his prodigious talent or its effect on his female listener.

"I was too surprised to say anything, and he didn't wait to listen. After that, he got kind of paranoid, I guess. Every time I'd be in the back pasture, he'd drive up and act like he was checking the fence line." Both Chris and Charlotte laughed at the thought.

"That was peculiar behavior for Henry" she interjected. "I don't suppose he ever fixed any loose posts or broken wire?"

Chris shook his head as he stretched the wire between two posts. "But it sure was creepy, like he was some shadow always lurking out there under the mesquite trees. Then last month he told me he was suing me. Said he'd talked to his nephew, who was a lawyer in Houston, and he was going to get his land for keeps legally."

Charlotte saw him looking for the wire cutters and was quick to retrieve them from beneath a lone prickly pear cactus. "Well, I guess there won't be any suit now. I can see why you want to get that fence line corrected as soon as possible."

"I'm doing it the right way, though," he assured her. "The surveyor is coming Wednesday, and I'm going to go to get the fence change certified on my deed, too."

Charlotte listened absently to Chris's proposed legal safeguards, but her eyes were on the disputed water. "That wasn't Henry's only tank, was it? Is that what you meant by the orneriness? He didn't even need it, did he?"

"No," Chris answered, almost vehemently.

"That's what my mother would call 'dog in a manger'," Charlotte replied. "You know," she mused, "it's kind of ironic. Henry bein' so mean or paranoid about water he didn't even need, and then he's washed away in a flood two or three weeks later. Poetic justice, I guess."

"It might not have been just meanness, though,' Chris pondered. "I wonder about that diabetes he was always mentioning. That might have caused his bad temper."

"Well, if he took care of himself the way he took care of his cattle, it's a wonder he lived this long. But I'm going to kind of miss him. What'll all of us neighbors talk about if we don't have any more Henry stories?"

Chris gave the wire stretcher a final turn and passed his forearm over his forehead. He spit casually onto the parched ground; and then winked. "Why Charlotte, you know there are already enough Henry stories to last until the cows come home."

CHAPTER 6

Water Witching and Other Surprises

CHARLOTTE LOOKED AT THE GRAY RANCH HOUSE with approval. The sagging floor had been restored to level, and sweet-smelling yellow pine had replaced rotten lumber, patching the old wood like so many bandages. The skeleton of a wraparound porch was emerging, and Charlotte could already envision herself sipping mint juleps on the front porch in the cool of an evening. Elroy had just cut the rough openings for the three sets of French doors that would replace the long and narrow windows in the living room, and a pile of scrap wood stood heaped next to each new portal. Something white in the pile nearest her caught Charlotte's eye. She carefully sorted through the dusty wood, avoiding bent and rusty nails to retrieve a ragged and faded piece of heavy paper. Charlotte's eyes widened and then she set to work in the other stacks of scrap lumber, sorting through them with the fanatic zeal of an Egyptian archaeologist exploring an ancient burial site.

After three quarters of an hour, she pieced together three pages of the latest Sears and Roebuck fashions...from the spring of 1916. Elroy sat in his truck, and smiled at her over his sandwich.

"They used about everything they could find to stop the wind from getting in back then," he explained somewhat surprised at Charlotte's enthusiasm over the dusty paper fragments. Charlotte held up one of her better finds, a 16x24 faded color sketch of two dapper gentlemen discretely eying a charming, seated female whose head, unfortunately, had not survived its entombment in the ranch house walls. They were quite elegant indeed in No. 325, the Single-Breasted, Fly-Front Overcoat and No, 326, the Three-Buttons Double Breasted Frock Overcoat. No. 325 had an especially devil-may-care image enhanced by his light walking can held debonairly in a gloved hand. Why, he even wore spats! No. 326 was more sedate. His gloved hands were all but hidden behind the full cut of his jacket, holding only a nondescript derby. The slacks were a conservative pinstripe, and the spotless shoes two tone with embedded laces. His look at the beheaded seated damsel was direct and a bit patronizing.

"I'd pick the one with the cane," Gary advised, pouncing on her thoughts in his mischievous way. Not only could he read her mind, but he also unerringly knew her choice in men!

"My daddy had spats like those," Elroy observed, catching Charlotte's enthusiasm in spite of himself. His lips curled in a boyish remembrance dusted off from over fifty years ago.

"You'd better put the pictures away for now, though, Charlotte. I can't find the water line."

Charlotte was jarred back to the present and very practical reason for the visit to the ranch today. It was not to glorify in Elroy's expert restoration, to indulge in imagined mint juleps, nor to become entangled in romantic triangles of sketched catalogue models from the spring of 1916. They were there to find the buried water line and extend it into the house. It should have been found easily; it had been capped off directly to the west of the house's back corner for easy access to the kitchen. This spot would soon be under a porch deck, probably tomorrow, considering the pace of that demon worker Elroy, who defied all the slow working stereotypes connected with being southern, or sixty. They must locate the pipe today.

The hard ground was pockmarked with ten empty holes.

Charlotte relieved her exhausted spouse and made three more craters before giving out to exhaustion, heat, and despair. She was leaning on the hated shovel for support when Elroy popped his head around the corner. "You having trouble finding that pipe?"

Frustrated nods were a silent response.

"Did you try witchin' it?"

Gary and Charlotte exchanged nonplussed stares. "Oh, you mean water-witching," Charlotte managed, her brain scrambled in the sun. "I don't know anything about that"

"Have a forked stick anywhere?" he asked timidly. None could be found. "Well, let's try some baling wire." Elroy sorted through the pile of scrap and debris and soon found two suitable lengths. He held one in each hand, the two wires pointing straight ahead and parallel to each other.

Gary watched without comment from the shade of a nearby mesquite. Elroy walked briskly past the notorious corner, dodging the many pits and piles of clay. Without hesitation, the two wires came together and crossed each other. Not at all surprised by this feat, Elroy approached from a different diagonal and again the wire lurched together.

"It's right here," Elroy announced, and he stuck a small piece of wood in the ground to mark the spot. Oddly enough, the stick was within a foot of at least three empty holes.

"Let's have a try," Gary suggested. Charlotte could only assume that his normal skepticism had been quelled by respect and admiration for Elroy, who had already began to work miracles with his carpentry. Desperation and the ever-present and unremitting sun probably played a role, too.

After three shovelfuls, however, the grim exhaustion was returning. Then a disc of white glinted in the sun like the eye of an awakening giant.

"There you have it," assured Elroy, not at all surprised, and he quietly resumed his measuring.

His scientific detachment a bit ruffled, Gary was nevertheless grateful to see results.

"Must be some reason it works." Elroy intuitively sensed the crushing blow he had dealt to academic thought. "It'll even point electric wire buried underground. Must break a wavelength or something," he soothed.

Charlotte, on the other hand, wanted no explanation. She relished the mystery like a Westerner falling under the spell of an exotic guru. And Elroy, with his craggy handsomeness, his lean, ascetic physique, and his natural humility, almost fit the part,

"Thanks, Elroy," Gary said simply, and he set to work with the shovel again. Ten minutes of digging exposed the buried plastic, and Gary was now ready to attach the extension that would bring the water line into the would-be kitchen under their future sink. A piece of rotted wood dangled to his right and seemed bent on snagging his arm with splinters. Quickly, Gary broke off the offending timber, but even in this, the old wood was obstinate. It broke unevenly, and as Gary seesawed the old nail loose, it somehow wedged itself behind the good wood next to it. With an impatient sigh, he reached into the wall to retrieve this last scrap, but his fingers did not feel the expected roughness. Instead he touched a leathery smoothness, curved and slightly resilient to his prodding. And then it moved!

Instant repulsion propelled him backward as if by an explosion. He looked at his shaking hand and hoarsely whispered, "A snake. There's a snake in the wall."

Elroy and Charlotte quickly flanked his prostrate form, and Charlotte went for a cup of water. Gary accepted her offering and drank sparingly, like the wounded soldiers he'd seen in World War II movies. So concerned was she over her husband's welfare that Charlotte did not at first notice the movement. Elroy pointed silently to the gap in the wall, and he and Charlotte watched in awe over Gary's shoulders.

Apparently, the snake had been just as repulsed be Gary's touch as he had been by its scaly skin. It slowly emerged from the jagged opening in an affronted stupor that suggested its annoyance at an interrupted slumber. Without a word, Elroy picked up the shovel and positioned himself precariously close, Charlotte thought, to the viper. The action was so swift she scarcely saw it, noticing only the devastating result.

The awakened snake had not even had a chance. With a single hammer-like blow, Elroy had smashed it, using the same sure and measured stroke he usually directed at wayward nails and such. Charlotte ventured cautiously closer, finding the carcass of the dead snake as fearsome as its earlier live version. She noted the triangularly shaped head and the small heat sensing pit just below its nostril, a wide chocolate gray band edged in white running diagonally down each cheek. The clay-colored diamond patches were outlined in the familiar wheat edging. The long and thick base of the tail and its circular black bands indicated it was a male. Were there any other snakes but this, Charlotte wondered as she confirmed her second close encounter with *Crotalus atrox,* the western diamondback rattlesnake. She recalled Damon translating from Latin that *atrox* meant frightful or grim. An apt name, she thought, as she tried to avert an involuntary shudder. This was truly a grand specimen, though, she could not help but note. The amazing factor was not its length--a healthy five feet--but its girth, which spanned a fully packed body three inches in diameter.

"I've got a friend who skins 'em for belts 'n hat bands," Elroy suggested, somehow managing to break the tense atmosphere. "He's all yours, Elroy," Gary decided. "You were the hero."

"But I didn't have to touch 'im," he chuckled.

"Well, he may be big enough for a hat band and a belt," Charlotte recommended.

"Well, I'll put him in my ice chest for now." Elroy used the shovel and gingerly deposited the specimen in his cooler.

"Better warn your wife before she unpacks your lunch things."

"That's not quite the same as cellophane, greasy napkins, and empty Pepsi cans." Charlotte laughed as she envisioned Elroy's unsuspecting spouse.

"Well, I'd better attach that pipe, or you'll never have your kitchen, Charlotte." Gary spoke as if they had merely indulged in an extended work break.

"Let's make sure he didn't leave no kin fold behind." Elroy returned from his toolbox with a flashlight. While he held the light, Gary poked and prodded. Charlotte, however, was not wholly satisfied with these measures and finally insisted they remove all three feet of wall beneath the window.

The larger opening offered a better view of the bowels of the old structure, and Charlotte was both repelled and fascinated by the assortment of serpent skeletons and shed skins nestled there.

One of these skeletons was museum quality with both fangs intact. Knowing that Damon would cherish this grisly relic, she grabbed a scrap of wood and carefully maneuvered the fleshless reptile toward her.

Gary and Elroy stared in awe at the grey/white bones that caught the sunshine. Suspended from the wooden scrap, they swayed and tinkled like the clay trappings of an innocent souvenir wind chime. Charlotte reached to touch the serpent's tooth, her hand somewhat slow and unsteady as she neared its sharpness.

"I'd hold up if I was you," Elroy cautioned more forcefully than usual. "Some of them fangs have poison in `em even after the snake's dead.'

"But this has been under the house for years..."

"Friend of my daddy's once nearly killed hisself from a snake tooth. He'd had a near miss with the fellow, a seven-foot diamondback. Even struck at old Vern, it did, but his boots saved him. Well, Vern killed it with a rock, smashed its head up pretty bad, but the skin was in good shape and he had a real nice belt made out of it.

"What he didn't know, on account of the head being so smashed in, was that the snake had lost a fang. It had gone into Vern's boot heel, but not far enough in to touch him. Buried in there so good you wouldn't even notice it. Vern never did, until his prize sow was a having trouble delivering her litter and he ran for the vet in a hurry."

Here the usually laconic Elroy paused dramatically.

"Put them boots on barefoot, and he was fretting so over his old sow that he didn't even feel the scratch when he slipped ` em on.

"Durn near unconscious by the time he got to the vet's. It was a good thing he was there, too, 'cause he was an old country boy, this vet, and he knowed the signs of rattlesnake poisoning right away. Had some anti-venom on hand, and to make a long story short, he saved Vern's life. Vern was delirious for days, and it was near a week later when they finally figured out how he had got bit, so to speak."

Elroy viewed his entranced listeners approvingly and chuckled while he watched Charlotte redeposit the skeleton under the house.

On second thought, let's not disturb sacred burial grounds," was all the pale would be archeologist could muster.

More searching with the flashlight revealed no new living or dead reptile relations, and thus convinced that the deceased serpent had led a solitary bachelorhood, Charlotte kept watch while Gary glued and capped the PVC pipe.

With the job completed, the snake safely out of sight and in fact, on ice, Gary began to relax, and his dry humor returned.

"For a while there I thought I might be joining Henry," he noted in a joke which Charlotte thought came too close to the truth. He smiled as he dropped this parting shot and ambled off to the barn to put away tools.

"I'd almost forgot. Henry's place is over yonder, isn't it?" Elroy paused for a moment in respect for the dead. "Well, wherever he is now, it'll never be the same again. Probably buying everyone drinks and tryin' to talk to a good-lookin' woman right now."

"So Henry was a ladies' man?" Charlotte probed, wondering why any mention of Henry now piqued her interest.

"He was married twice and had a woman in between. Lot of people talked about it at the time. She was a fine woman, though, and I think Henry really loved her. He'd a married her, too, I believe, but she was Black. People weren't so broad minded back then, you know."

Charlotte wondered if the local residents were any more broad-minded nowadays.

"She died some ten years ago, some say of a broken heart, but she had a son. Everybody knows he was Henry's pup."

"So Henry and this black woman had a child?" Charlotte felt compelled to translate Elroy's dialect into unbiased blandness.

"He lives right here in Structure. Name is Tyrone Cartwright, and you won't find a finer man or blacksmith anywhere around.

"Matter of fact, I think he keeps bees, too. He'd probably come clean out that hive of yours in the north wall. I can't work there 'til they're gone, you know."

Charlotte jotted down the name and promised Elroy she'd contact Tyrone about the bees right away.

"Does Tyrone know Henry was his father?" Charlotte asked.

"That I don't know. I never talked to him about it."

"Do you think he'll get Henry's land, but no--he's illegitimate," Charlotte answered her own question.

"Second ex-wife has title of the land," Elroy informed them. My nephew is county clerk, and he told me his office is processing the paperwork. She and Henry were co-owners, even after the divorce. With Henry gone, she gets all 100 acres, but I don't think she'll be needin' it."

"Why not?"

"Why, she's a high society Houston lady. Married into oil after she and Henry split up. A hundred acres to her is like dry hay to a cow grazing green bottomland. She don't need it or want it, I suspect."

"Why do you think she was still a co-owner, even after the divorce?"

"Henry was an easy going type, you know. He didn't bother about too many details. Probably just let it go--like he did his cattle and land."

The crunch of the tires on the dry Bermuda grass announced Gary and the Bronco, loaded up and ready to go.

"I'll call Tyrone about the bees," Charlotte promised Elroy as she got into the front seat. "Take care!" was her euphemistic reminder to watch out for more snakes.

"I want to see your new belt soon," Gary said through the rolled down window.

His teeth flashed in anticipation of his prestigious pelt, and Elroy nodded them farewell. Soon the only sounds were his whining saw followed by the steady staccato of his tireless hammer.

"A serpent's tooth," thought Charlotte, who had been even more shaken by her encounter with this skeleton than with either of the two living reptiles she'd come across, "so small, so delicate, so seemingly devoid of life, yet filled with a venom that was every bit as lethal as ever it had been. Waiting, hidden and almost invisible, for an unsuspecting victim."

CHAPTER 7
Mowing the Lawn - Texas Style

CHARLOTTE PULLED THE OIL STICK OUT and took a reading. It was full. Satisfied, she next hoisted the five-gallon gasoline container over the hood and listened as it gurgled into the tank. Before she was finished, the thirsty engine consumed a second five gallons. A quick glance at the encased six-foot shredding blade assured her that all was in order, so she stepped up into the molded iron seat and adjusted her Tri County Feeds cap and dark sunglasses. After starting the reliable engine, Charlotte glanced with satisfaction at the red and gray reconditioned beauty. It was reassuring to see something built the same year as she was running so smoothly and effortlessly. Nineteen forty-seven had been a good vintage year, she thought, for her and Ford 8N tractors.

She let up the clutch, adjusted the hydraulic to proper cutting height, and headed toward the back pasture. The engine droned noisily and jostled her gently as she moved over the coarse terrain. A wide swath marked her progress from the barn to the back pasture, a gray-green paleness indented in the taller grass. She looked behind her with satisfaction. Results were not so immediate or tangible in her classroom. She moved happily on, enjoying the rhythmic and occasional jolts like a salty seafarer glad to be back on-board ship.

Clearing the ten-foot opening that led into the back pasture, Charlotte turned the 8N sharply to the right to follow the outer fence-lined border, The grass flew like green foam in her wake, perfuming the air with its sweetness, landing in thick ridges like motionless waves. Soon, it would fertilize the land and make way for the new and tender growth the horses sought. While cattle would eat like lawn mowers, horses were much more fastidious and selected their forage with epicurean palates. The results were a pincushion pasture, where mounds of less succulent grasses were left to dry out and go to seed amid tender patches of greenery that were manicured like putting greens. Even preferred grasses, like common Bermuda, would be ignored if they grew too tall. Thus, the biannual shredding and the mindless pleasure of piloting the red and gray dinosaur machine through a sea of grass.

"You should marry a farmer, Charlotte," her father used to tell his nine-year-old daughter when he noticed her insatiable love and curiosity for the country. Those were times when women chose their direction in life through their husbands, like discriminating hitchhikers who peered closely at the driver before climbing into the front seat. But her love for learning had preempted the bucolic calling, and she had entered Indiana University on an academic scholarship to study English. The wooded campus had a sylvan charm that cast its spell over the naive freshman and the diffident graduate student who was anything but a farmer. Their initial courting was marked by heady conversation that lasted for hours, and the sense of trust and intimacy was immediate and steadfast. They shared a Spartan dedication to academics and spent many evenings cloistered in the sterile computer center, where her first love notes arrived over the IBM printout. This academic diligence was buffered by long rides in the local hills where promises and kisses blossomed in the verdant meadows, and after her twenty-first birthday, they were man and wife. His doctorate in psychology, a cabin in the woods, and a vivacious baby daughter were the fruits of those early years. The stilted house built on a forested hillside housed a stable below, and the happy threesome ended their days listening to the call of the whippoorwill accompanied by the steady munching of hay from below. Then the offer from Texas, the move to a land where winter's ice and snow could not keep them captive indoors, and the disappointing compromise of having to live in town. Land was not close at hand, as in Indiana, and a young career and family yielded no time for excess commuting.

So the dream slept while they put youthful energies into their own form of urban renewal. An inner city house in semi-decay was resurrected with the indomitable enthusiasm and man-hours that make supermen of husbands young and in love.

He sawed; she swept sawdust; they painted, scraped, peeled, sanded and shellacked until the bare bones of the turn of the century structure revealed the natural wooden charm buried in layers of paint. And then it was finished. He looked at his jewel and planned to bask in its radiance for a lifetime.

She, the Eve of womanhood in her, was not satisfied. But a bargain was struck. The second purchase, the ranch and the reclaiming of this gray albatross perched upon it must be her responsibility, must feed upon her creativity, must yield to her will and resourcefulness. And she'd surprised him by responding with a surplus of all four. Even plebeian jobs, like shredding the grass, she had relished. She drank up the heady perfume of the wild flowers and took from it a courage that guarded her territory from wasps and hornets with a militant zeal. She met fire ants and rattlesnakes and stood her ground. And, as he knew would happen, he too, her soul mate, caught the missionary fervor. So soon Charlotte had a partner beside her, once again digging, scraping, and sawing. But in the practical wisdom of middle age they had enlisted one assistant, the afore-named magician called Elroy. "No, Father," she answered aloud, "I didn't marry a farmer. I became one."

A bump and the clogging strain of the blades brought her quickly back from her romantic reverie. Charlotte looked behind to verify its cause and saw the expected sheared off top of the ubiquitous fire ant hill, its panicked inhabitants fleeing in defensive fury. She was glad not to be on the ground and in range of their lightning stings that warded off unwary trespassers. She had made four trips around the rectangular field now, and the cut perimeter framed the meadow in a green gauze ribbon of tidy grass. Already, the horses were sampling the gourmet fare.

Abras, the fattest of the bunch, stood alone in the higher grass the others disdained. He drew the thick succulent grass into his mouth, the great green bunches protruding from voracious lips, while thick foamy froth dribbled in jaded laziness from his muzzle. The delicate mares nibbled at tender short grass, testing each morsel with finicky delight. A jackrabbit fled before her, his mulely ears starchy straight as he anteloped across the field. Charlotte followed his bobbing tail as it zigzagged in frantic flight from the merciless swirling blades. He skirted the fence line and fled into the twenty-five acres that flanked their land to the north. It was still owned by Janet Loathing, the woman from whom they'd bought their land, and had been up for sale with almost every local real estate agent for at least three years. They'd been offered it recently, at a very reasonable price of $1,400 per acre, a clear one thousand dollars per acre below market value. But what did they need more land for, even at bargain prices. All their resources were going into this latest renovation, and the contented equines were plump testimony to the adequacy of their forty acres. She looked at the ugly scar of a road that cut an unceremonious and direct path across the bargain strip. Here was the rub. Henry Sweigurt, who had sold this land and theirs in a sixty-five-acre package to Miss Loathing, had retained this access strip for his heavy equipment.

The road to the front of his house afforded cars and light trucks, but I t was narrow and weak where it crossed the drainage ditch. Ms. Loathing, with all her big city polish and honey voiced smoothness, could not move him in this demand. She had tried selling the entire sixty-five acres and thus muting the access issue by bundling the ugly road into an unobtrusive corner, but she was unable to find any buyers for such a large package. Charlotte and Gary reasoned that she had made such a good profit from the sale of their forty acres--land prices had escalated sharply during her four-year ownership--that Ms. Loathing could afford to more or less cut her losses and let the orphan twenty-five live on the infrequent crumbs sent by the parade of local realtors.

But today, something was different. The darting jackrabbit had guided her eyes to the change. The access road was closed off, and shiny new fence posts glistened like new recruits guarding the old opening, their barbed wire arms locked in soldierly camaraderie. Now Charlotte remembered access rights were not always written into a deed, but often extended throughout the possessor's lifetime only. The orphan twenty-five without this ugly access strip now had an excellent chance for adoption. Maybe a wealthy Houston couple might now find them interesting.

Now just a narrow box of undisciplined grasses gloried in unruly display as the dry wind whipped through them. Charlotte turned the tractor toward the dancing patch of prairie and wished her ninth graders could be brought to order so masterfully, an evil thought that only a fellow schoolteacher could forgive.

She steered the 8N toward the barn, quite unashamed of her private uncharitable fantasies, and suddenly it struck her how Henry's death had benefitted several people with such immediacy. Chris Cavecross could not be sued for adverse possession, and he now gained land use and much needed water. Ms. Loathing now owned twenty-five suddenly very saleable acres. And an ex-wife in Houston, whether she needed or wanted them, now had exclusive title to 100 acres of what could again be good cattle land. For her, Corvel and Lucille too, there would be no more broken fences to mend, no more runaway calves to chase off like so many persistent flies. The flood tide, the rushing muddy water, had swept in some small, packaged treasures with Henry Sweigurt's demise.

CHAPTER 8

Land of Milk and Honey

A SHINY RED PICKUP reflected the morning sun as it climbed up to the house. The rounded fenders belied the youth of the fresh paint job, and the solid thud of the closing cab door told of the solid armor of its body. To lovers of vintage trucks, pickups that were made to do the job, this was a fine specimen. Gary, who scorned the eggshell exteriors coming from contemporary Detroit, walked over to admire it.

"This is really a classic," he told Tyrone, forgetting even to introduce himself.

"I' been workin' on it all summer," Tyrone smiled in undiluted pride. "Me and my boy, we reworked the whole engine. Tyrone Cartwright," he nodded as he extended a well-muscled brown arm in greeting. "And this is Fernando Munoz," he went on cordially as a wiry assistant emerged from the passenger side.

"I talked to you on the phone," Charlotte said in greeting as she neared them. She gripped Tyrone's firm hand and introduced herself and

Gary. Her spouse gave the truck a wistful pat, and nodded as he excused himself. The scrap timber had to be loaded onto a trailer and taken to the dump.

So this was Henry's illegitimate son. She noticed the handsome features, the high cheekbones and frank yet shrewd set of his eyes. The powerful chest and the carved sinews of the upper arms were those of a blacksmith, one with the strength to dominate his 1200 lb. clients. And the steady gaze that met hers showed a resolve and inner strength that would help him hold onto a rebellious hoof as it kicked back or reached skyward.

"You got some bees for us?" he smiled as he glanced toward the house. Fernando was already unloading a ladder and several clinking bottles from the pickup.

"I'd like to keep all the old wall boards, if possible. Can you do that?" Charlotte queried.

"I guess we can try. Maybe pull 'em out from the bottom only," Tyrone said absently as he poked a screwdriver in between the gray wooden boards, oblivious to the buzzing guardians that flew forth.

"You got some hives here," he concluded after getting positive results from two intersecting walls each fifteen feet in length. "Probably enough honey here to sweeten a city of sour women," he laughed, obviously enthusiastic about the challenge before him.

Tyrone was wearing his beekeeper's attire, the starchy whiteness of his garb in contrast to his mellow dark skin. The fitted headpiece hung down in heavy folds, making him look like an astronaut. He cut the waxed and papery hive with the same slow concentration of an Alan Shepherd, working with such care as to appear in slow motion. Indeed, as he descended the ladder with a section of hive carefully pinched between tongs, Charlotte said softly, "A small step for man. A great leap for mankind."

Fernando, similarly attired, received the specimen, which oozed with amber honey. He opened the drawer of the white wooden bee box, and soon the dislodged bees were leaving their old hive for this slick man-made bee condominium. Fernando worked with deft hands and quiet precision, his lean frame moving with grace as he maneuvered between house and pickup bed. Only a slight limp broke the flowing motion, a slight sideways action as he walked, a stiffness in the right hip. Now Charlotte remembered where she had seen him. Of course, Fernando, Fernando who worked for Henry.

They had even nodded at each other once or twice across the back fence.

"Fernando, didn't you once work for Henry?" Charlotte asked, her curiosity short-circuiting the usual social maneuvers that would normally lead up to this abrupt question.

"Yes, ma'am," he nodded. "I work with Henry." He politely emphasized the amended preposition. "Henry and me, we are partners. In Taylor, we have 52 cattles together. They belong to me now. Henry, he couldn't always pay me, so he make me a partner with the cattles. I even have papers to show it," he added almost defensively, as if he half expected Charlotte to demand tangible proof.

"I'm glad for you, Fernando," Charlotte assured him. "And that was thoughtful of Henry to put your name down as owner, too. Usually Henry wasn't that – " she searched for the tactful word – "careful."

Fernando nodded knowingly. "Henry, he is a good man."

Charlotte understood Fernando's grammatical limitations and his subsequent exclusive use of present tense, yet she felt a certain uneasiness in hearing Henry referred to as such. "Many peoples here, they talk about Henry and laugh at him. But he is always fair to me. With his sickness, he cannot do so much, though."

"What was Henrys sickness, Fernando?"

Fernando pointed to the growing stack of honeycomb fragments. "He has the sugar sickness. He no can have the sweets. Every day he must give him--" here he groped for the word and then, "mimed giving himself an injection. "Sometimes, he get dizzy out in the sun, so I tell him I take care of cattles in *el verano*, the summer."

"Then why was Henry going to tend the cattle in June when he..."

"Very strange, very strange," he said without looking up. "But the note, it says, he goes to Taylor. Maybe he is afraid I might not be able to get there from my house."

"What did the note say Fernando?

"Here, I have it," Fernando said. He reached into his back pocket and took out a worn leather wallet. The paper he extracted had been folded and unfolded until a network of wrinkles and creases stretched across it. Did Fernando keep it close to his bosom and read it daily in a sort of memorial religious ritual? The practical and intelligent eyes, however, showed no such superstitious or sentimental predilections. No, the note was more an enigma; a disquieting puzzle that disturbed him daily. The ragged parchment was roughly rectangular in shape with a torn upper right-hand corner. It read simply,

3:00pm
Gone to Taylor
Back Gate

"The back gate, we keep it close because the fence not so good in the front. But the back, it is under water when it makes bad rain," he explained. He paused and his features contorted in a brief show of emotion. "Why does Henry go to open gate? He knows I take care of it, take care of our cattles. Why does he not call me?" His pain and fondness for the old friend shadowed his face.

"Maybe he tried and couldn't get you." Charlotte proposed.

"No," Fernando answered, familiarly--as though he went through this same dialogue every night with himself.

"I open gate in morning when it begins to rain. Then I go home and call Henry to tell him the cattles, they are safe. But he is not home, No. If he call me, he get me. I am at home all the time until

4:30. Then I go to check on Henry, like every day, when I feed the chickens. This is when I find note."

"Fernando, over here," Tyrone called. His booming laugh told that it was no emergency, but Fernando was over to the house in all speed, anyway. Hanging precariously from the series of boards that were hinged from the house was the most enormous section of beehive Charlotte had ever seen. This was the main store hold for the honey, and the glistening 4x8 section of moist amber was full to the brim. The trophy could not be taken as a whole, but Tyrone had to share its unique beauty before cutting it. The two men worked with skillful efficiency to remove small rectangles of sweetness.

"I never seen so much honey all in a bunch," Tyrone exulted. "Even my Mozelle won't know what to do with it all. Ma'am?" He turned his triumphant grin to Charlotte. "Can I slice some of this up for you? There is nothing finer than natural honey; and these wild hives have a special sweetness. I see you have a good stand of clover in that pasture over yonder." He nodded toward the wild section that skirted the corral, the violet blossoms of wild clover now fading to a dusty pink. "There ain't no better honey than clover honey made by wild bees. Some say a spoonful a day will cure you of allergies, too," he continued, and Charlotte recognized the same fascination and wonder that led her to lecture captive audiences about the biological habits of local reptiles or the unique ancestry of the Arabian Horse.

"I'd love some, Tyrone. But what can I put it in?"

"What about this?" Fernando was carrying the large red and white plastic ice chest.

"That'll do fine," Tyrone told him. You just cut those sections small and put 'em in jars in your refrigerator, ma'am. Just keep the hive in there too. It'll take a while for the honey to come out, an' that hive won't do no harm. Kinda gives it the genuine touch, too. We used to use the comb for chewing gum when I was a kid. Never knowed there was another kind."

"We got to scrape them boards, now, and then spray 'em good with bee repellant. I don't use no poisons, ma'am, jest this repellant. It should keep 'em from coming back."

"I'll bid you good-bye now, ma'am. Sometimes them bees don't like this scraping and the repellant. It puts 'em into a rage sort of and I might have to leave in a hurry."

He tipped his beekeeper's helmet and went to work. Charlotte, feeling guilty about deserting her spouse, returned to the scrap heap and set to work. She pitched the wooden cutoffs onto the trailer like a child making a mountain of wooden blocks. Gary, more the engineer than his frivolous child-spouse, carried his stacks of lumber in tidy bundles, which he tucked into corners and openings with glove-tight precision. Somehow this hodgepodge wooden tower worked--it had a strange beauty and structural soundness that combined the careful and the carefree, precision and playfulness, much in the same way their marriage did.

Charlotte tossed her last scrap with a tired sigh and saw the red truck rumble down the hill toward the road. And in the wake of the hastily departing pickup, a buzzing escort voiced an indignant protest.

CHAPTER 9

The Eagle's Nest

GARY STEPPED BACK TO ADMIRE his creation. The last coat of paint had dried to a powdery blue that complemented the darker hue of the trim. Semi open louvers gave it a clapboard primness that contrasted with the glittering pyramided roof. And atop it all a prancing copper stallion turned in the breeze and literally became what the ancient Arabian called this noble beast, "a drinker of the wind."

It had taken one week for Gary to build the cupola after he had been inspired by a high-priced model at the lumberyard. But perhaps the most difficult part lay ahead. Today, they must dismantle the old brick chimney that perched above "kitchen" and "living room" to-be, occupying what was to become a five-foot opening between them. Instead of merely patching the roof, in this cavity they would put Gary's created cupola, a blue jewel with echoes of New England. He had even included a wizard touch--a soft blue light that would glow cool and pure between the louvered openings, a sapphire beacon to welcome them home at eventide.

He called to Brandy and Damon, who sat astride the pitched roof on either side of the chimney. "Okay, begin the demolition." Soon the sky rained bricks; gray and tan pieces rolled down the tin roof like Texas-sized hail. Charlotte waited for the avalanche to end and began to sort the ancient bricks into neat stacks. Visions of a future patio motivated her throughout this mundane chore.

Gary walked onto the new low-pitched porch roof, a piece of *terra firma* next to the steep pitch of the original house roof. He climbed and scooted to the metal summit and calculated several mysterious measurements. The children were coaxed down from their perch, and the whole family labored to hoist the 200 lb. creation up to "the eagle's nest." First it was mounted on top of the venerable 1969 International Scout that they pastured on the ranch. An all-out effort landed it on the porch top, but it was a mad scramble to get it astride the high roof. Charlotte knelt on all fours on the porch top to give Damon a leg up. Brandy, her mother's daughter in terms of heights, watched nervously from below, alternating between warnings and words of encouragement.

Finally, the blue jewel rested on the peak, the triangle cutouts of its base creating a kind of trigonometric saddle for this strange metal beast it must straddle. In a few moments, it was temporarily secured to the peak, and Charlotte began to resume breathing. Gary and Damon slid down to the almost flat porch roof, and presently, all four Choirbys were on the ground.

But the critical slant of his heavy Croatian brows told Charlotte that her perfectionist husband was not satisfied. Wooden slivers would be needed to wedge under the cupola, which to Gary's gaze was askew. It would be her task to sit atop the gentle slope of the porch roof and patiently hand needed tools to the two-man crew astride the peak. Brandy would be on-hand to report whether the cupola was remaining level, a task that presented more problems than one might think.

Brandy's immediate response, given her feminine tendency to worry about loved ones on precarious perches, was to give affirmative and enthusiastic reports. However, if the cupola were secured to the roof out of plumb, the whole task would have to be undone and done again. This second option undercut her easy optimism, creating ambivalent and ridiculous responses, such as, "The cupola's level, but the roof isn't."

Perhaps it was fatigue or the altitude, but somehow Gary accepted this dubious affirmation, and he and Damon began to fasten down the cupola.

"At least we don't have to contend with the bees," Charlotte sighed as she handed up a large screwdriver, "Tyrone and Fernando must be the Pied Pipers of honeybees."

"Can't believe Tyrone is Henry's son." Gary laughed. "It contradicts everything I've ever learned about genetics and heredity." He paused to grunt over the final turn. “That man loves to work; he lives for it.”

“Did you see his eyes glow when he saw the size of the hive?” Charlotte chimed.

“And everything finished to the last detail--the scraping of the wax, the bee repellant, and coming back the next day to re-nail the boards.”

“Not like the first beekeeper we called. He took his honey and left, never mind that two walls still were solid hives.”

“And not like his father at all,” Gary repeated.

“You know, Gary,” Charlotte mused, “the Henry Fernando described didn’t sound so bad, though. He made Fernando a partner in his cattle operation. And Fernando almost idolized him.”

Gary bent to his side to swoop up the next proffered screw, looking like a polo player leaning into the ball. Charlotte, who was cautious even on the safe porch roof, was amazed at his balance and dexterity. “Fernando is the first person I’ve talked to who wasn’t happy that Henry died.”

Charlotte was on tiptoe to meet his extended hand. “It’s more than just grieving, though. He’s bothered about some things...and, you know, so am I.”

“Like what?” a voice from afar asked, and Charlotte was reminded of Damon’s presence.

“Well, the trip to Taylor, first of all. Fernando says that he did all the cattle work during the summer months, because Henry had diabetes and became dizzy in the heat.”

Gary’s rolled eyes indicated his disbelief in Henry’s disability.

"So why would Henry suddenly become so conscientious and independent? Why would he go by himself in a rainstorm to open up a pasture gate for cattle when he knew that Fernando was taking care of them?"

"It doesn't sound like the Henry I've dealt with," Gary returned.

"I picked up four cattle skulls from his property," Damon reminded her.

"Right!" Charlotte was building momentum now. "And another thing that no one has mentioned until now. Why that short cut route to Taylor? It had been wet all month and had rained all morning. No one in their right mind would have tried the dirt underpass that day."

"No way. We almost cracked up when it was barely sprinkling," Damon remembered.

"But the question remains, my dear. Was Henry ever in his right mind?" Gary, almost finished with his task, was beginning to take an interest in Henry's death, in his own dry, sardonic way.

"We're ready for the calking gun, Brandy," Gary yelled down.

Brandy ascended the ladder to the porch roof armed with her caulking gun. "How do we know that Henry was going to Taylor, anyway?" she queried.

"From the note Henry left Fernando," her mother answered. "It said that he'd gone to Taylor and mentioned the back gate. He'd written it at 3:00 p.m."

"Why the note at all?" probed Gary in between careful applications of the sticky white glue that snaked from the "gun" like a cautious serpent. "Why not just call Fernando?"

"That bothered Fernando, too," Charlotte remembered. "He was home all afternoon, too. If Henry had called, he would have reached Fernando.

"Maybe he panicked when he heard about the flooding," Brandy chimed in from below. But even the trusting Brandy could not envision Henry panicking over discomfort or even peril facing his cattle, and her voice did not carry the ring of truth.

"Some interesting points," Gary conceded, "but probably they could all be explained simply...if only Henry were here to tell us." One by one, he handed the tools down first to Charlotte who then passed them down to Brandy. Damon, however, chose a more creative method. Instructing Brandy to stand clear, he let gravity do the work, and suddenly the hammers, screwdrivers, wooden slivers and such, were skimming down the aluminum roof like it was one giant slide, and bouncing to the ground with dusty landings.

The tools were then carefully packed away while Gary and Damon stretched their kinked muscles. As Gary stepped back to inspect his work, Charlotte watched his face contort in disbelief.

"It's crooked! The whole cupola is crooked!"

And without asking, Charlotte knew exactly what they would be doing tomorrow.

CHAPTER 10

Going, Going, Gone

"LOOKIE HERE, LOOKIE HERE!" the auctioneer croaked as his assistant struggled to hold the unwilling fowl for all to see. "What a prize specimen. And this here prize guinea is only one of, how many, Shorty?"--a pause while Shorty attempted to count the free birds while keeping the one captive--"Thirty-two, nearly three dozen prized guineas, all healthy, as you can see by our wigglin' friend. How much for the lot of 'em? Who'll give $50 for this flock of beauties?"

There was a large crowd assembled at Henry's farm-estate sale: an assortment of working farmers, their wives and restless children, and some others who ventured forth from town.

The first bid came from a large man who looked like he'd been born in overhauls. A bulbous nose stood out from the craggy and weathered features that marked him a man of the soil. He was bettered by a middle-aged gentleman, his stylish jeans and dapper western shirt topping boots that were definitely too new and shiny.

Probably an accountant newly enamored with rural settings. And fancy fowl would just complete his romantic notions of the country. He was probably envisioning fresh country eggs when another bid topped his.

"Used to raise guineas myself," Corvel confided to Charlotte. "They was almost as pesty as a committee of church women, and as gossipy, too. Their cluckin' tongues never did stop a waggin'."

"And was they dirty!" Lucille added. "I'll never forget the smell. I couldn't eat no eggs nor chickens for months, even after they was gone. I guess I learnt to hate them when I was a kid. My chore was to gather the eggs. It was bad enough to go in that hen house of a hot, muggy summer morn, but one day I almost fell off in faint."

Corvel's eyes twinkled as he finished his wife's familiar tale. "You ever smell a bad egg, Charlotte?"

"It's worse than a skunk's scent, kind of like bein' trapped in a sulfur pit," Lucille recalled. "I was sick to my stomach for the whole day." And indeed her memory was so vivid that Lucille looked like she was about to relive her experience.

"I see your truck has a new paint job," Gary noted, eager to seize upon a subject devoid of gastronomical connotations.

But instead of the proud response she expected, Corvel's answer was a meek and almost sheepish, "Yup."

"Why don't you tell him why we had the $250 paint job, Corvel?" his spouse teased.

"Well, ya see," he began slowly, "I had a little smash up at the Type store. Backed into a car as I was leavin'. It was parked over to the other side, where nobody ever parks. I wasn't expectin' it, and I couldn't see a durn thing, with the rain so thick."

"It was the day of the flood, the day Henry..." Lucille left a delicate but meaningful pause. "Corvel done the right thing, though. He left a note on the car, even took down the license number."

"I never seen that car before. A real fancy model, foreign made and sporty. I knowed it didn't belong to any of them boys I was havin' a beer with, but I asked inside just to be safe. Had a Houston sticker, I believe."

"And you know, Corvel never has heard from the owner." "Left my name and insurance company on the note, too." "Well, anybody with money to drive a car like that, mebbe they don't need no insurance check," Lucille laughed.

"I was thinkin' of trying to write 'em. I even got the name and address from the Department of Motor Vehicles, but..."

"I told Corvel," Lucille finished for him, "I told him he done his duty as a citizen, no need to do more."

"Been over six weeks now and no word," Corvel continued. "Never seen that car around here since, neither."

"Why look at that lamp," Lucille interrupted. She pointed at a particularly elaborate specimen representing a young peasant girl in a vivid palette of colors, carrying a basket of translucent fruits atop her head. Obviously the colorful assortment of bananas, pears, oranges, and apples glowed in incandescent glory when the beauty was electrified. But Lucille was enraptured not by the luminescent fruits, but the shade, a magnificent testimony to its genre. Gauzy layers of draped chiffon bowed and curtsied in the scalloped edge, which ended in a grand profusion of fringe and colored beads. And all was perfectly preserved in its original plastic protector. When it was discovered that there was a perfect pair of these beauties, her enthusiasm reached new heights, and Lucille bid in almost religious fervor.

She returned, proudly bearing one maiden with all the careful devotion of a mother carrying her first newborn. Behind her, with a less sentimental attachment to his burden, followed Fernando with the other. They were carefully deposited in the front seat of the pickup, leaving room for only one rider.

"I guess I'll have to be ridin' in back," Corvel groaned.

"That's what happens when you go smashin' up cars," Gary kidded.

"Or was it you who was smashed?" Lucille ventured in the casually insulting tone that a wife can only dare when she knows it isn't true.

"Now, if there was anyone who was snickered," Corvel laughed, "it was ol' Henry. He was a bit shaky when he left Type that day. He even slurred his goodbyes. But I thought at the time that he was just unsettled bein' in the company of such a classy woman."

"So Henry was at Type store that morning," began Charlotte.

"With a classy woman?" finished Gary in disbelief.

"Yeah! They was sitting at the same table talkin' kinda close and serious, I guess. Seemed like they knowed each other a while. Must have come together, too, 'cuz they left together in Henry's truck."

"I told Corvel it was probably one of them out of town-landlords that Henry farmed for. Probably coming in from the city to check on her business."

"What's the matter, Lucille? You can't imagine Henry knowing a good-lookin' woman on his own?" Gary chided her, knowing they all doubted Henry's potential as the romantic leading man.

"Fifteen years ago, he was a different man, before he lost all his land and money," Corvel answered almost sadly. "He was good lookin', and charming when he wanted to be."

Now it was Charlotte's time to be drawn from the conversation by the magic of the auction. Unlike Lucille, she was not drawn to over refined and rococo flamboyance usually relished in rural trailer homes. Her downfall, and happily, Gary's too, was the opposite. "Things that looked like they needed to be carted away," her father had once chided, those were the pieces that called to her.

Now she was bidding on a cast iron tub with tremendous claw feet.

"You going to use it to water your horses?" Corvel asked, never in his right mind thinking she would want to bring the antiquated relic inside.

"Why, this is going to be our bathtub, Corvel," she answered without flinching at his preposterously practical suggestion.

"Oh, and I thought," twinkled Lucille, "that it'd be perfect for making a batch of homemade mustang grape wine."

Now Charlotte was not unconditionally opposed to practicality, especially if it had a hint of romance or adventure.

"You're right, Lucille. We'll make the wine in here first, and then use it for a bathtub."

"Kind of a baptism for it," Gary suggested.

"Or you could jest take a bath in the mustang wine," Corvel chuckled, proud of his witty return from the scorned stock tank suggestion. "These city people were a type all to theirselves," he thought.

Charlotte and Lucille left their laughing spouses and returned attention to the auction, each eager to find more prizes to top their recent buys. The next item on the block, however, called to Gary, not the women. It was Henry's old pick-up, a rusty-gray heap of tin dating back to the forties. Like a loyal dog, it had been a one-man truck with a gearshift so elusive and complicated that only Henry could drive it. But the motor was strong, and solid and the body had in strength what it lacked in looks. Henry used it anytime he had farm work or cattle business. Many the calves that had ridden home from stock auctions in its large bed. The number of hay bales and grain bags it had toted could only be guessed at by the assortment of dried stems, seed, and grain that lived in its crevices, sometimes sporting green growth after a rain.

Charlotte looked nervously at Gary and saw glazed eyes and a slight flush in his cheeks. He was beyond her intervention now, and she settled herself into acceptance of the iron albatross, to lonesome Sundays of grease smeared "widowhood," to her role as getter of wrenches and sockets, to countless trips to auto parts stores until she was on a first name basis with the condescending clerks. She even managed a brave smile when the auctioneer congratulated Gary on his buy, and she then walked briskly to inspect her inanimate rival.

"It's a good thing Henry was driving his new pick-up when he was swept downstream," Gary rambled on, oblivious to the rather callous reference to Henry's death. "This old timer is worth ten of those new jobs."

"You know, it was strange, though, now that you mention it."

Charlotte said. "Why did Henry take the new truck to a job he knew would be dirty? We all knew he always used this truck for ranch work."

"Don't make too much sense to me neither," Corvel replied. "He always bragged on this truck, how it'd go anywhere and do anything--his good luck charm, he called it."

"He could have used some of that luck that day, couldn't he?" was all Charlotte said. She glanced reflectively at the modest house just fifty feet away. Gray asbestos siding covered the rectangular frame, and the same faded blue curtains hung in the windows. Strange, and almost disloyal, she thought, that the house should look so unchanged, as if it hadn't even noticed the loss of its owner. She guessed that everything in the house had been herded to the auction block by now, but Charlotte still had a desire to look inside.

The grimy window didn't offer a very good view, but she was able to clean off a portion with her hand. No, not everything was gone; there was still an assortment of Henry's belongings scattered inside. These were the items the Houston Auction Company deemed as trash, the junk that even auction zealots would reject. There was a dingy couch against the wall, with sagging springs and a worn floral fabric. A Naugahyde armchair patched with silver duct tape kept it company. The kitchen was entirely bare, except for the grease coated cabinets and linoleum counter. Two glasses, half filled with dark liquid, sat near the stained enamel sink, which dripped steadily. Near the back door, a dirty rain slicker hung on a hook, its fluorescent yellow the only bright note in the drab room. That was all.

Charlotte closed her eyes and tried to remember a different Henry--the Henry of fifteen years ago; handsome, flamboyant, and even charming, Corvel had said. But the lonely gloom of the house haunted her, and she was unable to conjure up any such vision.

CHAPTER 11
A Trip to Town

CHARLOTTE LOOKED DOWN at the railroad yard and cotton gins beneath the paved bridge. Cotton gins and the railroad, the very core of life to small town Texas. Next in Taylor came the honky-tonk section, that strip of cheap saloons and beer joints interspersed with a few wooden frame houses and small but not thriving businesses. There was Shanty's, a ramshackle bar that promised on its signboard, "We'll Never Tell," and the White Elephant Room, with a large wooden cutout of the pachyderm above its portals. "What are you looking up here for?" was carefully lettered below the beast, disclosing the owner's strange sense of humor. Hattie's used furniture was a fenced yard with a makeshift roof. And piled upon each other was the ugliest assortment of junk ever assembled. Even if a gem were spotted within its confines, it would be impossible to get within ten feet of it, let alone uproot it from the snarl of debris. Pat's used motor equipment housed an assortment of grimy lawn mowers, while its side yard displayed old farm equipment put out to urban pasture.

Now the old business retail strip began, with the Calico Cafe and Mercantile Printing, joined by the dream window of wedded bliss called Eloise's Bridal Shop. Before they could pass on to the newer retail establishment, to the McDonald's, Pizza Hut, and Walmart, they veered to the left, toward the John Deer Shop, west of town.

The outside lot was filled with all that technology could do to take some of the drudgery out of farming. The most important feature was the enclosed and air-conditioned cab. There one could sit astride his mechanical mount without the brutal sun racking his brains. He could be free of the dust and pollen that followed a tractor like a magnetic cloud, and he could laugh at the tropical temperature without. And, yes, in some very top line models, he could even soothe his ears with the strains of stereo music.

But Gary and Charlotte's goal was a more modest version of the air-conditioned cab, a canvas canopy that would be the farmer's version of a parasol. Before they got down to this rather plebeian purchase, however, they could dream. They could climb into the green cab: they could sit in the softly upholstered seat, hold the smooth steering wheel in hand and imagine the strains of Mozart enveloping them in classical embrace.

And Charlotte had another ritual she performed at all tractor dealerships. She sorted through all the free brochures until she found those on hay and small grain production. These she studied with academic zeal, her goal: the perfect pasture, with perennial grasses. She was currently developing her plan to grow both a summer and a winter pasture on the same ground, to have a new carpet of green that would replace the summer growth after it fell to frost. The key was how to do it without the need to plow deeply. She read on...

"Charlotte, which color do you like?" Reluctant as she was to leave the delightful reading about the comparative merits rye verses oats and the relative yield and temperature tolerations of each of these cool weather grasses, she nonetheless closed the pamphlet and walked to the counter. The choice was between red and blue.

"Well," Charlotte weighed aloud, "the red certainly matches the tractor trim, but it is so apt to fade. Blue, on the other hand, will capture the essential hue of the gray chassis, but it's not really a match."

The young man behind the counter kept a very straight face as the all-important color choice was decided. He even acted as if all farmers weighed the hue of tractor canopies with such single-minded effort.

"This here red don't fade that much, ma'am," he interjected helpfully, and thus the choice was made. Red it would be. A well-coordinated tractor ensemble was, after all, essential for the up-and-coming land baron.

"Hello, ma'am. Do you like the honey?"

Charlotte turned to face Fernando, who was behind her in line.

"Why, hello, Fernando," she smiled. "Oh yes, the honey is delicious. It was almost worth the trouble with the bees."

"The bees, they are all gone now, yes?" he queried.

"We haven't seen any since you and Tyrone were there," Charlotte reassured. "By the way, did you go to the auction last week?"

"No, I no want to go back to Henry's place now. With him gone, it is very sad. I remember my friend too much, and I not like to see his things sold, sold to someone who never knows him."

There was an awkward pause while Charlotte wondered if she and Gary should feel guilty for purchasing the tub and truck. Then she remembered something that had been bothering her.

"Fernando, didn't Henry always use his old Chevy pickup when he was doing farm chores?"

"Sure, he only drive the new truck when he go to town." He paused knowingly. "I too wonder why he drive the new truck to Taylor that day to herd the cattles."

"And he was wearing his good boots, too. Did you know that Fernando?"

"No!" His eyes opened wide and then narrowed. "Something is very strange. I know that from beginning when I find note...

"Could he have been drunk?" Charlotte ventured boldly. "He was stumbling when he left the Type Store earlier that day."

"Henry, he does not much drink, only one light beer. He cannot because of his sickness. His is careful of that, I know. Never have I seen him *boracho ...* drunk."

"I was at the auction," Charlotte confessed, her mind running back to her last image of Henry's house. I saw something in his house, and it didn't strike me at the time, but now I think it is strange, too. A yellow slicker was hung on the wall in the kitchen. Was that his only rain coat?"

"Yes, the yellow coat with the hood," Fernando nodded.

"Why would he leave that when he would be going out in the rain? And the glasses, too..."

"I know," Fernando interrupted. He needs his glasses to drive, so why do I find them in case next to note?"

"What?" asked Charlotte, who had been referring to the drinking glasses and knew nothing about eyeglasses.

"I find his glasses in kitchen when I find note," Fernando repeated.

"Next," the clerk said, and Fernando moved up to the counter to place his order. Charlotte waited briefly, eager for more bombshells of new information, but she could see that Fernando had some complicated questions about an automatic feeder, and she also saw Gary eying her significantly from the front seat of the Bronco.

"Goodbye, Fernando. We'll talk again soon." Charlotte squeezed his arm and left. She decided not to mention any of this to her logical and skeptical spouse. He would only offer a rational explanation, which, right now, she did not want to hear.

The ride back to the ranch was ten miles, just long enough for Charlotte to scan the day's paper. She read the usual stories of politics and violence, the self-righteous editorials, and the more direct and enjoyable letters to the editor. She even had time to unscramble the word games, take a skeptical look at her horoscope, shake her head over the outrageous but motherly Dr. Ruth, and peruse the Dear Abby column. She read with personal interest the article about the new airport to be built in nearby Manor, Texas, and all the predictions of spectacular land prices in the area. Charlotte supposed their land would be worth more now, since Manor was only some fifteen miles away, but she was not particularly enthusiastic about urban sprawl or noisy airplanes creeping or flying toward her precious forty-acre plot.

The headline "Arrested Man Sues Police," did not even seem strange to her, and it was only because she had read everything else of interest that she even noticed the article. The caption, "Suit says suspect was ill, not drunk," caught her attention, and she read on:

> A 34-year-old South Austin man is suing the Austin Police Department for arresting him on a charge of public drunkenness when, the man says, he had passed out on the street from insulin shock.

She skimmed the incidentals and then studied the medical explanations:

> People suffering from insulin shock may have slurred speech, poor coordination, and lose consciousness, an Emergency Medical Supervisor said.

"It fits," she mumbled aloud. "At least one piece of the puzzle is solved."

CHAPTER 12

A Trail Ride to Type Store

"DON'T FORGET TO BRING SOME CASH for drinks at Type," Charlotte reminded Gary, as she took out the electronic clippers. She wanted Abras to look perfect before the skeptical scrutiny of the local Sunday cowboys at the Type Store and roping arena. She shaved the silver mane from the ears four inches down his long-arched neck in a typical Arab style, the purpose being to accentuate the refined crest and throatlatch. Fancy Dan foppery, probably, and the local quarter horse enthusiasts would not be impressed. But didn't they spend long and sometimes dangerous minutes patiently plucking tail hairs from their mounts? The thinned tails were supposed to emphasize the muscled hindquarters of their horseflesh, and Charlotte smiled as she compared the relative anatomical fixations of the two diverse breed enthusiasts. Somehow, the head of a horse was much more appealing than its hindquarters, but she would never dare to suggest such to the local ropers.

A final brushing and Abras glowed an almost blue-grey with dark areas around nostrils and eyes that showed his black Arabian skin underneath. She climbed atop her English dressage saddle and dusted the black riding boots. The German riding pants were a new skin that moved easily with every flex, and she was especially pleased with the suede-lined section that stretched across any part that touched the horse or saddle, providing a Velcro-like adhesion to her mount. True, this suede appendage did look somewhat strange when she was afoot rather than astride, but Charlotte was prepared to brave curious glances directed at her suede swathed derriere and practiced a defiant gaze that usually transfixed giggling ninth graders. She hoped it would have the same effect on the local ropers at Type Store.

Gary looked especially handsome in his dressage outfit, Charlotte thought, kind of like Prince Charles at a polo match or the sketched insignia on Ralph Lauren cologne. But while this attire was synonymous with genteel masculinity in Europe, South America, and even certain of the more civilized areas of the United States, she was not quite certain how it would be perceived at the Type Store.

"Wait just a minute, honey," Gary sang in an unnaturally saccharine voice. "I'll be right back." When he emerged from the barn, Willie Nelson had eclipsed Prince Charles, and the Gary that accompanied her wore Levies over his Tony Lamas, and rode a quite respectable looking western saddle on his prancing mare. In fact, he even looked askance at her circus style tail that was carried with habitual flamboyance, high and arrogant in the breeze. They rode in silence along the road, the horses eager and excited to be out on the trail. Charlotte was lost in thought, and Abras knowingly took advantage of her reverie and snatched great tufts of Johnson grass into his bridled mouth, eating with the careful tediousness of a teenager in newly acquired braces. His patient manipulations with one particularly huge shaft finally awakened Charlotte to her negligent horsemanship, and she leaned over to pull the grass from his gluttonous grasp.

"I was wondering when you'd notice," Gary laughed at his wife" who usually took great pride in mastering her defiant gelding. "You've been a million miles away for the last quarter of a mile."

"Yeah, I've just been wondering," she replied reluctantly, uncertain whether or not to share these intuitive misgivings with her rational spouse. "It just doesn't add up. Right from the beginning it hasn't been right."

"You're mad because I changed to jeans?" Gary asked, sheepish over his collapse to conformity in riding apparel.

"Oh, not that," Charlotte smiled sympathetically. "No, about Henry, I mean. His death--there's nothing right about it."

Gary was about to say, "There never is," or some other pompous cliché, but quickly swallowed the easy truism. He knew that his wife, for all her whimsical and romantic notions, was in essence a very logical and intelligent creature--"much more intelligent than I am," he often reminded the children when they didn't show her the proper respect. He took pride in recognizing her intellect, which she often kept camouflaged behind an unpretentious openness of character. "What isn't right about it, Charlotte?"

"Well, first of all, there were the boots. Even Lucille couldn't understand why Henry would wear his custom-made alligator boots to round up cattle in a soggy pasture." She looked for a response, but Gary was only an alert listener at this stage.

"Then there was the message to Fernando. Why didn't he phone Fernando? Or better yet, why would he even go, when Fernando was already taking all the cattle responsibilities during the summer anyway?"

Gary looked at her shrewdly, his eyes slightly narrowed. "Go on."

"And when we bought Henry's old truck, remember we commented that it was strange that he had used his good Chevy instead of it that last day."

"And why did he take the short cut?" Gary continued, catching her missionary zeal. "You told me that even a little rain made the temporary detour around the bridge nearly impossible."

Charlotte nodded, remembering the tense moments when she and Damon skidded their way up the red clay temporary road that crossed the run off. "Why, by early afternoon on that Saturday, the water would have been flowing through there. No one would even have even *attempted* crossing there.

"And I didn't tell you about the glasses?" Charlotte confessed. Henry's glasses were on the counter when Fernando found the note at 4:30. Fernando told me that when we saw him in Taylor at the John Deer dealership."

"And Henry needed his glasses to drive, I suppose," Gary concluded.

"Yes, that's what Fernando said, at least. But the funny thing was that when I started talking to Fernando, I meant something else entirely . I was asking about the drinking glasses on Henry's counter. I just wondered who his guest was. And why his only raincoat was left hanging on a peg in the kitchen."

"Wait a minute. I think I know, Charlotte. Remember Corvel joking about Henry being tipsy when he left Type Store? That might account for everything. Why he made such bad decisions about the boots, the truck, the glasses..."

"Gary, he wasn't drunk, and he didn't leave Type Store alone."

Her tone was so sure and serious that Abras mistook it for a reprimand and stopped dead in his tracks. She patted his neck and gently squeezed her legs against him. "Fernando swears Henry was never drunk, that he only would drink one light beer."

"Probably had to restrict his alcohol because of the diabetes," Gary suggested.

"Yes, and that has me thinking." Charlotte then told him about the article she had read in the paper, and how insulin shock often caused the appearance of drunkenness.

"Okay, same thing then, Charlotte. Henry isn't drunk, but he's out of control because of insulin shock. The results would be the same; his judgment is bad and he..."

"But you're forgetting the second part of what I said, Gary. He didn't leave alone."

Now it was Gary's turn to stop his horse, almost if he couldn't think and ride at the same time. "You mean, if he really was bad off, his friend, the mysterious classy lady, should have been there to help him."

Gary's mare, surprised by his unconscious tug on the reins, moved her head up and down, seeming to affirm her rider's logic. Abras answered by blowing air through his nostrils, as though he, too, was caught up in the mystery of Henry's death.

"Are you saying his death was not an accident, then, Charlotte? That he might have been murdered?"

"You know Henry has never been the most popular person in these parts. And look at all the people who gain from his death."

A particularly aggressive little mixed beagle ran after them in fierce patrol of his road frontage, and the riders maneuvered their dancing horses onto neutral frontage before continuing.

"Chris Cavescroft gets his own stock tank with no hassle of Henry's adverse possession court case. And Janet Loathing is suddenly free of Henry's access rights and the ugly road that made those twenty-five acres unsalable."

"And Fernando now owns fifty-two head of Brangus," Gary continued. Not bad for someone who was not even a documented worker until a year ago. Oh, I know that fifty-two head of cattle isn't a fortune, but men have killed for less."

"Maybe, Gary, but Fernando really loved Henry. He's probably the only one who mourns him. And anyway, it's Fernando who first got me feeling uneasy about all this."

"He wouldn't be the first murderer to shed alligator tears," Gary countered and then he ruthlessly analyzed the murderous instincts in all the rest of their neighbors. "And did you ever think of Tyrone? Here Henry is his father and supposedly Tyrone's mother died of a broken heart. That's pretty strong motivation on an emotional level. Vengeance is sometimes stronger than greed..."

"Well, I guess I'd have to include his second ex-wife, then, too," Charlotte added. "After all, she gets sole possession of the 100 acres, but I don't think Houston oil money is seriously..."

"Houston oil money isn't what it used to be, Charlotte. And 100 acres within fifteen miles of a new airport might motivate some to murder.

The Type store and contingent rodeo arena were not far now. Charlotte could make out several horse and stock trailers parked by the side of the road, the patient and unflappable quarter horses gently swatting flies as they stood tethered to their rigs. They were very nonchalant as trailers, other horses, and chap clad cowboys maneuvered around them.

The two high-strung Arabs, however, were excited by the new sights and crowd and sidestepped at 45-degree angles along the black top. Charlotte was reminded of the intricate dressage step, the side pass, which took years to teach, but apparently the locals were unacquainted with its intricacies and not duly impressed, or at least their sneers would indicate as such. Then, from over the bend, Corvel's huge combine tractor came adorned in full battle dress, its side discs fully extended and its engine issuing the equivalent of a bugler's charge.

Abras and Capzara, used to the routine tractor work done alongside their pasture, accepted the metal chargers with aplomb, but the barn-raised cow ponies had never met such a road warrior, and suddenly the tables were turned.

The calm quarter horses were now in all stages of irrational rebellion. One buckskin was seated on its haunches, pulling with all its might against its lead rope. The robot roper in the area ceased its predictable lope and was suddenly a rodeo saddle bronc. A Shetland pony, previously the trusted placid carrier of toddlers and even infants, had been incautiously tied with a leather rein, which it now dragged on the ground as it ran out of sight down the road.

Sitting tall in the saddle and observing these catastrophic happenings with complete equanimity, Gary and Charlotte rode their two now docile mounts up to the parked John Deer giant. And with a final audacious triumph geared to avenge months of unmouthed ridicule, they tied the calm desert steeds to the very blades of the mammoth tractor.

CHAPTER 13

Mustang Grapes

CHARLOTTE CLOSED *Home Winemaker's Handbook* with a grim smile. Grapes grown in New England, the author's locale, ripened in the pleasant Indian summer days of September and October, and the amateur wine enthusiast could harvest his white or red jewels with the pale rays of an autumn sun as his companion. He could gather the whites--Delaware-- a suitably native name for potential "wine light golden in color, characterized by a flowery-fruity flavor" or Diana--"aptly named after the Greek goddess of the moon," or even the more sophisticated French American white varieties such as a Seyval Blanc--"very delicate, of superb bouquet, and a delight to drink." Or if his fancy ran to the more robust reds--as Charlotte was told brunettes like her favored--he could gather Bacchus--the name itself suggesting riotous and pagan abandon or Zinfandel--which produces "wine of fine quality and a brilliant color, with sweet bouquet, rich body, and good flavor." Or finally, for those eschewing the heathen overtones of

Bacchus, Mission--California's oldest grape, reminiscent of the long history of wine and its religious overtones, recalling monks in their sacred duty as winemakers.

But here in Texas, it was a different story. Her fruits of the vine were not goddess-grapes like Diana or sacred mission varieties, brilliant Zinfandel or even exotic Bacchus grapes. The harvest in Texas reflected, in its own way, the Lone Star heritage, its rugged and unrestrained atmosphere, its own brand of wild abandon. Today, Charlotte was going to harvest wild mustang grapes that ripened, with typical Texas perversity, in the heart of the summer, in the brutal heat in early August. And indeed, her mind-set and gear were much more akin to the frontier wrangler going to round up wild horses than to the sophisticated and scholarly gentility that harvested Seyval Blanc in New England's autumn.

She had borrowed Corvel's huge cow hide boots, donned her oldest blue jeans and cotton shirt, and dutifully anointed herself with a combination of sunscreen and Kerosene according to Lucille's time honored formula. Like any true inhabitant of the Sunbelt, every inch of skin was covered and protected from the sun. Only sun worshipping adolescents or vacationing Northerners sported summer tans. The true Texan, if he were able, remained pale in the summer and only sought the sun between October and April.

The rest of the clan appeared similarly attired. Damon looked fashionable in his ragged jeans, tattered t-shirt, and mirror front sunglasses; Brandy was a punky version of a Princess Ann in English riding boots, stone-washed denims, and a garish pink t-shirt from her California boyfriend, saying something outrageous like "Surf Naked." Gary wore his ranch uniform of boots, dilapidated Levi boot-cut jeans, and burgundy t-shirt, appropriately splotched with paint that perfectly matched the blues and reds of the ranch house, as well as all those other colors which had been tried and rejected. It was, in fact, a chaotic but accurate chromatic history of the ranch house painting, which had occupied most of his July.

Brandy and Damon carried the plastic ice chest, while Gary and Charlotte balanced the aluminum stepladder between them. Charlotte noticed that the motley splatters on it matched Gary's shirt perfectly.

Damon, the lightest and leggiest of the group, was stationed atop the aluminum perch, where his efforts to reach tantalizing purple bunches produced postures that ranged from Baryshnikov to Lucille Ball, Danny Kaye, and the Keystone Cops. He handed his sticky treasures to Brandy, who deposited them in the rapidly filling chest. Those overripe specimens she duly culled by popping them in her mouth, much to the protest of the master grape harvester risking life and limb to deposit them in her greedy little hands. Gary and Charlotte were wisely removed from the sibling squabbles, wandering boldly into the dark thicket where the succulent bunches grew in wanton and almost decadent lushness.

"You don't really think Henry Sweigurt was murdered, do you, Mom?" Damon asked, trying to hide his curiosity in amused cynicism.

"I do!" asserted Brandy, which now guaranteed that Damon would play the devil's advocate.

To squelch what she knew was merely a vehicle for but another brother-sister argument, Charlotte listed her suspicions in logical order: Henry's failure to wear a) his working boots, b) his rain slicker, c) his eyeglasses, and his strange choice of the new truck over his working pickup were clipped off briskly. Damon listened politely but seemed unconvinced.

"All that I can understand--mistakes made in a hurry, in a panic," Gary's voice drifted in from the thicket. "But it's Henry's character, his personality that doesn't fit. If Henry let his cattle die of neglect here in his own pasture, in his own back yard, literally, why would he drive ten miles in bad weather to help some cattle way over in Taylor?"

"He might have been lazy, but he wasn't dumb," Damon added, in spite of himself, "and I know he wouldn't try to take the short cut or even go near the closed bridge in a storm."

"Remember how bad it was when we brought the horses back from Henry's pasture that day, Mom?" Brandy remembered. We left here before noon, and it was already flooding the ditches and washing onto the roads then."

"What time did Henry put on his note?" Damon asked.

"Three o'clock," Charlotte remembered. "The flooding must have been pretty bad by then, because I know it rained all afternoon."

The ice chest was now full, but the vines were heavy with fruit. Noting the vast difference between the empty cooler and the filled one, Charlotte wisely opted to get the car and drive the harvest back to the waiting claw foot tub. She and Brandy deposited the glistening grapes and went back for what ended up as four more batches. The heat and effort soon sated their curiosity about the demise of the previous owner of the relic claw foot bath, and the foursome was content to talk of more pressing matters, such as where to go for an air-conditioned lunch in Taylor--MacDonald's or Wendy's.

Returning somewhat refreshed, they sat in the shade of the porch and began the sticky job of removing stray stems and washing the mustang grapes. Charlotte used the time expediently and reviewed the rather brief description of crushing grapes.

> If you start with fresh grapes, of course, your first task is to extract the juice. To do this, you will require some type of crusher--unless you are willing to resort to the time-honored method of crushing them with your feet.

What followed were tediously detailed accounts of crushers--from commercial contraptions to homemade varieties ranging from hoppers and serrated rollers to the more modest potato method.

To Charlotte's chagrin, there was nothing in any of her three books detailing "the time honored way." But here they were--the tub swelling with ripe orbs of sweetness, her tired crew poised and ready for direction, and Charlotte's hastily checked out reference sources were a bust. She looked to her sunbaked family, whose purpled clothing and heat-flushed skin resembled their fruitful harvest, and Charlotte knew she must improvise. Why, she'd seen grape stomping done in countless Cecil B. DeMille movie epics.

"First we must put on shorts and wash our feet and legs three times." This ritualistic three just came to her and seemed to fit all the pagan-Christian magic associated with this drink of the gods. Somehow, she vaguely remembered something disgusting about the foot oils enhancing the flavor of the wine and had a momentary urge to suggest that Damon not participate. After all, even wine could be too pungent. But her son was washing his feet with all the fervor of a young intern, and she didn't have the heart to disappoint him.

"Should we towel dry between washings?" he asked, already caught up in her imaginary instructions.

"No, that re-contaminates your feet," she improvised. Just rinse with water and walk on these spread-out towels to the tub," and Charlotte made a terrycloth royal carpet leading from the hose to the tub. The two teens were shy at first, but soon disbanded any attempts at dignity. By the time Charlotte left them in Gary's care, she was reminded of times ten years earlier, when he sometimes supervised bath time.

"I'll be right back. I just have to borrow those bottles from Lucille."

Lucille had an assortment of glass and plastic bottles lines up on the shelves in her shed, and Charlotte was able to garner several. She borrowed Lucille's utility knife and sawed off the upper half of a ten-gallon spring water container made out of plastic. Topped with cheesecloth, which she had bought in quantity, this would be a dandy primary fermenter.

Lucille had the perfect solution for a non-detergent wash--she merely put the whole assortment through the dishwasher cycle without soap. While they awaited this twentieth century appendage to the ancient art of wine making, Charlotte and Lucille chatted comfortably.

"Corvel, can you believe them kids is over right now a-stomping them mustang grapes," she chuckled.

Corvel, his blue jeans discretely loosened under his overhanging shirt, padded into the kitchen. Now Corvel, whose idea of cocktails was limited to long necks and aluminum, good al' Texas sippin' whiskey, and on special occasions "bourbon and branch water," didn't quite understand the mysteries of wine or wine making. He couldn't see why people would spend hard earned money on the sweet bubbly in stores, let alone go to all this trouble to make it. But he had a genuine affection for his somewhat eccentric gentlemen farmer neighbors, especially the children whom he delighted in showing his newborn calves and baby goats.

"I'd like to see that!" he said, almost like a tourist ready to purchase a ticket to some carnival freak show.

"Well, come on back with me, Corvel, and you can see the wine stomping at close quarters, "Charlotte answered. "By the way, can have that number I asked for, Corvel? It's just a hunch, but I'd like to check it out."

"Corvel complied after rummaging through several drawers, finally finding it thumb-tacked on the bulletin board. During the search, Charlotte entertained the neighbors by telling about her shock when she found no directions on how to crush grapes the old fashioned way.

They were still laughing over her shared secret of the improvised "stomping directions and washing ritual" when they stepped onto the shaded porch to join a napping Gary.

"Don't fall asleep, Gary," Lucille warned. "This is a very delicate process."

"Takes lots of supervisin'," Corvel added.

"Well, I'm so good at supervising, I can do it with my eyes closed, Gary quipped.

"Here, I brought you something real to quench your thirst." And soon the would-be wine makers were toasting their vintage with something brewed rather than aged.

The tub of grapes now reduced to purpled pulp, Charlotte watched as Damon and Brandy hosed themselves off. They played in the water just as they had in the tub, and Charlotte was struck by the inborn affinity between children and splashing water.

"Do the people that own Type store have any children?" she asked.

CHAPTER 14

Mulling it Over and Baiting the Hook

HER LAST WEEK OF SUMMER VACATION, and Charlotte decided she would enjoy herself. After all, the last few weeks had been hectic, although she had been witness to a magnificent transformation that reminded her of the first time she saw an orange and ebony monarch butterfly emerge from its dull grey cocoon. So it had been with the ranch house.

July had seen the weathered grey exterior turn cool shades of blue complemented by the redwood-stained porch deck. And there had been moments of adventure in painting the old metal roof in rustic red. She recalled Gary's ingenious methods of securing himself and his ladder on the high-pitched peak--his wooden angled extension to the ladder that clipped it to the apex while the ladder lay sprawled down the other side like a sled poised to go down a slippery slope.

And there were the out of the way spots where Gary lay flat on his back like a modern Michelangelo, or balanced with merely a single foothold while he clung to a friendly piece of wooden trim, his other leg askew, moving counterpoint to paint strokes like a brush bearing trapeze artist.

Then there had been the three days of 102-degree temperatures which had been allotted to wiring the house--from the attic down, since there was not enough space to work from below, not to mention the reluctance to inconvenience other creatures which perhaps still inhabited the lower recesses of the house. "An agriculturally altered microhabitat," her *Texas Snake Encyclopedia* had called such structures as their ranch house had been. The hay stored within had attracted any number of mice and birds, and the snakes had found a new Eden, so to speak.

Charlotte had banished them, all creatures great and small, who had over the years taken up residence in the ranch house. The bees had been persuaded to follow Tyrone to new quarters, and the sleeping serpent had fallen to the mighty hammer arm of Elroy. Uttering high-pitched reproaches as they scurried away, all the mice had left with the old hay. The solitary barn owl that habitually left his attic dwelling upholstered with snake skeletons left over from midnight suppers, had been regretfully evicted with the new second floor windows. Charlotte had been comforted, however, when she saw him roosting one starry night in a venerable oak tree that overlooked the stock pond like an aged Daphne at last free from the lusty Apollo.

The most persistent had been the mockingbird who insisted on maintaining a nest in the parlor, which was firmly glued to the mellowed rafters with a mud paste. The nest was twice removed, but built again within the day. It was spared a third destruction when a nestful of fragile eggs was discovered. So work could continue, a window was left open, and the devoted mother made her entrances and departures in style, through the colonial style wooden window, which received coats of paints and varnish in between maternal visits. The babies, duly hatched and taught to fly--an event which took only a day, as observed by Brandy and Damon from a discreet distance--the nest was left empty at last, and the window could now be closed. But the nest remained attached to the rafter, and was treasured like some jeweled broach left by a former resident, still glowing softly from an abandoned closet corner.

The kitchen had been August's challenge. The decision to angle the stove from the far corner had taxed Charlotte's vague recollection of sophomore geometry, but her calculations had been correct, and the wooden cabinets, ordered as premeasured modules, fit perfectly against the almond oven. A closeout on hand painted Mexican tile had captured their imagination, never mind that there were only nine of this style, sixty-three of that, or forty-two of another. Charlotte had spent hours with graph paper, only to abandon this academic pursuit, which was a second too recent reminder of geometric proofs. Instead, the family living room became the test counter and any number of patterns were tried and tested on the large brown rug. Finally, she was able to weave all the odd lots into an almost mystical Persian carpet of blues and amber; earthen flowers dancing over bold geometric splashes of cobalt blue. The nine blue stars were molded together in a tribute to Texas that was the focal point of the corner-angled stove. And all this time, Charlotte had checked on the mustang wine, fermenting on schedule in the 65-degree coolness of the old cistern. She hoped it would be ready for Oktoberfest, and the special barbecue celebration she was planning for that date.

But today would be a celebration in its own right, for civilization had arrived at the ranch in the form of indoor plumbing. She tried the shiny new mirror aluminum sink, letting the pewter water splash loudly and gurgle down the drain. Next, she ran childlike to the claw foot tub, emptied of its mustang grapes, and now newly enameled and ready to surround aching bones in a tubful of hot suds. An ancient walnut dry sink had been refitted with an ivory bowl and running water, and its scarred patina seemed at home with the aged claw foot bath. Best of all, however, was the pride of Sears and Roebuck's catalogue--not 1915--but 1988. Charlotte pushed her glass against the door-front refrigerator panel and received a clunking flow of rounded ice cubes. Now she pressed her iced glass against the adjacent lever and watched it fill with refrigerated water. She remembered the long months of carting water in five-gallon containers, and then later, quenching her thirst on the warm liquid that flowed from the green garden hose. But today, today she lifted chilled liquid to her lips and sipped it with the same awe and gratitude that Rudyard Kipling's soldier felt for his Indian water boy, Gunga Din. With a final salute to the Sears Roebuck miracle, she set down her glass and picked up the fishing pole.

The back tank was a serene turquoise green, clear and sparkling so the spongy algae was a sharp three-dimensional image, a kind of textured quilt that lined the shore. Minnow sized perch darted in and out of a hidden opening, like the deft fingers of an old woman tightening a stitch or mending a tear. The green and yellow blur was at first part of the crazy quilt's pattern, but soon came into focus. Charlotte's heartbeat in rapid palpations as she realized that she looking down directly at a fourteen-inch bass. She blinked incredulously, and he was gone, a phantom fish in which even she did not believe. Just when she had convinced herself that this was a heat induced mirage, he appeared again, retracing his course through the tufted algae only to disappear within its folds. Soon he was back, patrolling his territory with military detachment and almost bellicose defiance.

It must be protecting his brood or mate, Charlotte realized, and recalled fisherman's tales of bait taking frenzies brought on by reproductive reflexes and territorial defenses. She envisioned the iridescently dappled yellow-green body shining in the sun as she reeled it in to shore. Would this be dinner, or should she consider having it stuffed, the first of their stocked bass to be brought in--and by a woman, at that.

The sun was low in the sky as Charlotte slunk back to the house, the empty pole carried haphazardly at her side. So much for the fallacious tales of mendacious fishermen. She cursed them and the insulting bass that seemed to move from detachment to defiance to derision as the hours had measured his regular patrols.

She had locked the gate and was headed for home in air-conditioned comfort when she noticed the youngsters splashing in the plastic wading pool next to the trailer. At least they were having fun their last week of summer vacation. Charlotte turned the car to the left and stopped at the adjacent Type store.

She held the cold aluminum against her still flushed cheek and relished the wet coolness. Sipping slowly and deliberately, she drank the nutritionally empty beverage like a tonic, soon feeling somewhat refreshed and almost able to forget about failed fish fantasies. As she walked to her car, Charlotte almost tripped over a red and blue beach ball that had strayed from the plastic pool. She picked it up and carried it over to the children, first rinsing the dust and dried grasses off with the hose. It was now clean but sagged in the pathetic way of all beach balls in their programmed life cycle of twenty-four hours. Like a veteran mother, she tried to re-inflate it, an effort that produced a glimmering orb that she knew would be spent by the time she reached the highway.

Temporarily, however, she was a hero, and Charlotte used this exalted status to ingratiate herself with the young bathers.

"This pool is great," she began, admiring the solidly formed plastic sides. "Not at all like the miserable ones I had when I was your age. Ours had sides that were like inner tubes, and you had to blow them up, just like this beach ball, but it took a lot longer."

"And did they get holes in them as quick as our beach ball?" lamented the older boy, who was already noticing the gradual deflation of their only pool accessory.

"Just about," she sympathized.

"This pool is new--only one week old," the little sister interjected. "Before this, all we had was Mama's garden hose, and she didn't liken us to use it on account of all the water."

But I bet she didn't mind when the water was free--when it fell free from the sky, and you could play in the rain," Charlotte ventured in a surprisingly natural way.

Both children, however, seemed to ignore this rather beautifully crafted transition, lost in a splashing spectacle which wet Charlotte and threatened to end in the inevitable choking gulps, gasps, and tears. Knowing time was of the essence, she scrapped her more subtle efforts and asked directly.

"Were you playing out in the rain the day of the flood, that day Mr. Sweigurt was drowned?"

Not at all put off by this bold non sequitur, the little girl nodded. "Yes'm, but Jimmy here, he wanted to watch *Flintstones.*"

Several minutes more of chitchat were interrupted by their mother, who peeked her head out the door to call supper. Charlotte smiled in a friendly way that tried to indicate that she was not a child molester, but she was somewhat uncertain of the success of this communication.

During the drive home, she turned the radio off and kept a silent vigil with her own thoughts, even breaking forth into a spoken dialogue with herself at times.

Damon greeted her at the door and was, in his emerging manhood, insulted by her question.

"What time does *The Flintstones* come on television on Saturdays?"

CHAPTER 15
Rites of Fall

THE ROOM WAS HOT, stuffy, and filled with a pungent odor of anticipation that hung heavy in the air. It was the insufferable deadly calm that preceded a storm, when the still humid air pressed in upon you, refused to dry the moist film that beaded under soggy clothes, and made the mere intake of a breath a chore.

Then the storm broke loose, signaled by an ear shattering drum roll of thunder and the cymbal crash that followed. It rolled in in red and white fury, streaks that bounced and ricocheted in a riot of red, a cascade of crimson, and a whirl of white, like the foam of an angry sea. The waves of color reached a crest and receded in a pattern that finally distinguished ten separate shapes, synchronized still, but now emerging as distinct entities.

They moved with geometric precision, the discipline of sharp movement and statue stops replacing the chaotic wind-rushed entrance. The red and white sea, now suspended in movement defined itself as linear shafts of color that now began to wave--flag like-over the flushed skin. The cadence began, the stomping rhythm that called forth an echo ten times as strong, and ten pairs of expectant eyes topped smiling lips that began the ritualistic chants and gyrations.

The pep rally had begun. Charlotte located a familiar silhouette moving proudly in the starchy newness of the cheerleader's uniform and felt a moment of maternal pride. Never mind that hers had been a high school experience somewhat more shrouded in academics, the sedate lines of symphony black and white her uniform, and that the thrill of performance had been on the concert stage rather than the playing field. She still knew the surge of adrenaline that set a heart thumping in those moments behind the curtain, the steady shaking that seemed not to issue from unsteady knees, but from a strangely vibrating floor, and the final triumphant breath that was at last deep and satisfying, that enjoyed the audience's applause, but really was responding to its own inner critic, the still voice that accepted quality or nothing.

Reminiscence aside, Charlotte now settled back in the dented metal of the folding chair, seated in the segregated enclave of faculty members who cheered with awkward self-consciousness, remembered fanaticism, or dignified aloofness reserved for post adolescents held captive at such primitive rituals. There was a particularly unsettling part of the assembly that came with repeated awkwardness each week--the cheer off, wherein each group (9th, 10th, 11th, 12th graders) or affiliation (band and team members) vied with each other for the spirit award, generally based on volume and vehemence. The dedicated end by now slightly deaf diehards who loyally attended each pep rally, presently now rose in masochistic union for their attempt at glory. The short clad coaches were their centurions, seated in a front row of chairs, their muscled legs and torsos looking somehow incongruent under the balding scalps, greying temples, and weathered visages. Their testosterone inspired pitch was deep, masculine, and confident, and formed the bulwark of the faculty assault, Charlotte and her colleagues leading a strong soprano effort, enhanced by assorted tenors and bases from the math and sciences. Once, an all-out effort consisting of flash cards, tempera painted banners, strange hats, bells, and various degrading devices such as megaphones, pom poms, and miniature banners, had gained them the coveted spirit stick, a Pyrrhic victory that they had not sought to repeat. And there were those unfortunate instances when common sense had been held captive and Charlotte and other gluttons for punishment had participated in various faculty skits, another of the primitive tribal rites of secondary schools. Sadly confirming the penchant for self-punishment that characterized high school teachers, she had at different times been a raisin mouthing, "I Heard it on the Grape Vine," a ridiculously inauspicious homecoming queen in blackened teeth and peroxide wig, a caricature of the stereotyped old maid school teacher, a Romanian Gypsy who sold curses and fortunes, and most recently, a representative of the latest

Rock phenomenon, the rap singer. Decked out in rolled up jeans, cocked baseball cap with brim upturned, adorned with belts, chains, and a shiny polyester jacket, Charlotte had riveted the audience with her jive rendition of "License to Ill," a performance enhanced by authentically arrogant "rap" postures taught her by Damon, a fierce aficionado of the genre. In an inspired moment she had even "beat boxed" into the microphone, creating a series of rhythmic outbursts of air that mimicked a snare drum and thus earned her the permanent epithet "Chillin' Choirby," a title she tried to underplay as she indoctrinated freshman into the rigors of grammar, or inspired juniors with the subtle nuances of literature.

Her ears ringing, Charlotte left the pep rally, momentarily washed free from collective twentieth century neuroses and anxieties, and temporarily in touch with the primal rhythms of pagan innocence and violence that are a savage vestige in all humankind. She was certainly grateful that first period was her planning hour, as she hated to face thirty young bodies in various stages of recovery from blood fever, and try to teach them the accumulated wisdom / pedantry of the ages.

She returned home just after 4:00 p.m., hoping to watch the adventures of Captain Kirk and his new crew as they "went where no man has gone before," but was disappointed instead by the repulsive game show, *Anything for Money.* A perusal at the T.V. weekly showed times and programs completely jostled in that September ritual known as fall programming. This was the same television schedule where she had been disappointed to find *The Flintstones* scheduled at 4:00 p.m. after Damon's insulted silent response had sent her to another reference source to seek the Saturday schedule of immature animation now scorned by her adolescent. But now it dawned on her with a glimmer of hope that the June airing of *The Flintstones* had not been at 4:00 p.m. as this fall lineup had stated. She must call the station and find out.

As Charlotte hung up the phone, the hint of a smile teased her lips, but her eyes had the blank stare of a computer monitor flashing, "Please stand by--complex calculation in progress." It was another hour before she emerged from the privacy of the bedroom phone, and her reddened ear showed marks from the plastic receiver. That evening found Gary and Charlotte at the football game, where the faculty section was sadly contingent to the brass section of the school band. Their successful passes and runs with the ball were punctuated with cymbal clashes until Gary was traitorously hoping for the rival's victory. But he was soon to find that lost yardage or rival offensive movement brought an equally lamentable response--the brassy "charge" bugle and a cacophonous choral response. Ears ringing, Gary grabbed his Nikon and sought refuge down on the field, at one with a group of similarly camera burdened fathers who assumed ridiculous yoga-like contortions to get just the right framing of their progeny. Some doting fathers even sweated under the yoke of heavy video cameras, their sagging shoulders a badge of proud parentage. Indeed, so single were they in their photographic enthusiasm that one might have mistaken the group for a visiting entourage of Japanese tourists.

It was now half time, and the band and drill team were performing intricate maneuvers on the field. Charlotte, scanning the crowd, caught the familiar lanky profile and still colt-like amble of Shannon Crate. A fierce adherent of militant patriotism, Shannon had been the creator of an outrageous political posture that most mistook for genuine fanaticism. But Charlotte had seen through the guise easily enough, and knew that Shannon would have been his daguerreotype if he had lived twenty years earlier, easily exchanging his designer sun glasses for Ben Franklin lenses, his button down neatness for a wrinkled T-shirt, his clean shaved skin for bearded griminess, and his close-cropped stylish hair for long, rebellious locks. What mattered was the effect, the shock value, the impact his preconceived outrages had on his liberal minded and middle-aged teachers. So she had not been shocked, as most others had been, by his decision to attend a prestigious but politically leftist college, his law school years at an Ivy League institution that was a "hot bed of communism," and his rise to the Houston District Attorney's office which was headed by an aggressively liberal D.A. Shannon would achieve impact through achievement now, not guile or planned outrages, and since achievement didn't have time for fanaticism, he had stripped off his assumed zeal like an outgrown set of clothes.

There was still the same unassuming manner, the reticent warmth behind the eyes, but it was a more comfortably assured Shannon that greeted Charlotte tonight. They laughed and chatted without the awkwardness that often characterizes time lapsed meetings with suddenly grown up former students, as this was the real Shannon that Charlotte had always known and seen, even before he did himself.

After talking intensely throughout the colorful parade of halftime festivities, Charlotte scribbled something on the program back, smiled good-bye, and returned to the anticipated musical onslaught of the second half.

The evening ended with a closely fought victory, underscored by more musical excess, and a tired couple walked to the parking lot, glad that the opening ritual had been completed. Now the school year had officially started; the final clash of the cymbals had been like the rupture of overflowing champagne that bubbled and sparkled to Christen *The 1998 Academic* ship *of State.*

And so the days drifted together. The brutal sun was still a formidable enemy at four-thirty when Charlotte walked to the school parking lot, but its dominion was briefer each day now, and soon only gentle warmth greeted her air-conditioned flesh as she entered the faculty lot. She had calculated the first set of report card grades and was pleased not only with herself for finishing before the weekend, but also with her students, who had not done badly at all. It was in this mellowed mood that she entered the living room, in the midst of a firm fatherly tirade directed at Brandy. The subject was the telephone bill.

"But Tanya lives in Dallas, not Houston, Daddy. And I only called her once since cheerleader camp. She called me the other times."

The heavy Croatian brows were still unmoved and the stony expression lingered.

"I made the Houston calls," Charlotte intervened, and faced her angry husband with her most melting smile.

"I do think the weather's cooling off, don't you? Maybe the wine is almost ready," she sputtered on lightly.

"Oh, and I'll need this," she said sweetly, lightly taking the portable phone from the table and leaving an open-mouthed Gary in her wake.

CHAPTER 16

Wine at Last

THE COOL OCTOBER AIR played with clouds of smoke that issued from the black iron grill. Plump sausages sizzled gently, while silver wrapped ears of corn steamed, and bacon-spiced beans waited patiently on the warmer shelf. Gary, appropriately identified as head cook by his checked apron and white chef's hat, was monitoring the sausages carefully, jabbing wayward links with his pronged barbecue fork every so often. Brandy had colorfully lettered "Chateau de Charlotte: 1988" with characteristic flamboyance and was now arranging delicate wine glasses on the gate-legged porch table. Damon arrived with the old metal cistern bucket, newly cleaned and bright like a retired soldier recalled to active duty. Charlotte followed with a gallon jug of purple liquid that she carried like a proud but apprehensive mother. She carefully cradled it in the old bucket, while Brandy and Damon blanketed it with iridescent crescents of ice. The hand -lettered label was annexed with blue yarn tied in a neat bow, and all three stepped back to survey the effect with critical and then approving glances.

Lucille and Corvel arrived next, with a warm bundle of fresh bread tucked under gingham cloth, its rosemary aroma mingling with the smoky sweet October night and the juicy sputters of fat that struck the grill with great fragrant bursts. Corvel's contribution was set on the porch--a crockery jug for those who preferred their refreshment strong, smooth, and aged in oak.

Tyrone, his wife Zabrina, and their son came next. She was a beautiful woman, with high cheekbones, a lean athletic frame, and the natural aristocratic carriage of a goddess. Her deep-fried biscuits matched her beautiful tawny skin, and the dark amber jars of honey glowed like gold.

Fernando followed shortly, looking very prosperous in his designer type jeans and western shirt. Freshly polished boots caught the rays of the setting sun glowing like magic slippers from countless fairy tales. His bundle of steaming homemade tamales, while not usually part of the German Oktoberfest tradition, supplied the perfect appetizers, and were so different from the dry store-bought variety as to defy namesake. Charlotte thought them the perfect collaboration of the German, Mexican immigrant influence on Texas, a precedent setting blending of cuisines, while Damon showed his approval by pilfering one on his way through the kitchen.

Old-fashioned German potato salad, hot, with the red skins still on the potatoes, smelled of hot smoky slabs of bacon and sweet sour cream vinegar dressing. Chris Cavescroft, with his ever-present dip of snuff underlip, carried his contribution to the red picnic table. His wife, Sue, followed, with a jar of homemade cucumber pickles, their emerald liquid glistening in the sun.

Elroy was last to arrive, a still warm Dutch apple pie balanced in each hand, which his shy wife apologized was "as close to German" as she could get. More chairs were brought out, and the sounds of quiet laughter drifted across the rolling pasture, where the horses stopped and lifted their heads at the unaccustomed sound.

A glance at her watch and Charlotte gave the prearranged cue to Damon, who complied with her strange request, though she refused to explain its cause.

"Why," he thought, as he lugged the portable television to the bench he had set in the yard, "would she want the T.V. here?" He remembered overnight stays and lonely afternoons when football playoffs had to be missed because no television or phone was allowed at the ranch. He adjusted the attached antenna, but just smiled and shrugged at all the adult questions.

"A toast," Charlotte began, when she saw that Brandy had distributed the glasses, all of them resplendent in various hues of sun dappled purple, violet, burgundy, and lavender, except for Carvel's, which was a distinct shade of pale amber.

"A toast to Elroy," Gary interrupted, "the magician who turned a junk heap into a house." A shy smile and the reply,

"You're pretty mean with a hammer yourself."

"To Tyrone and Fernando," said Brandy, "Without them, the bees would be here, not us."

"And to Mother," Was it really Damon's voice she heard? "The only one crazy enough to think we could do it."

Everyone had duly drunk after each tribute, and only a sip or two was left in each vessel. Corvel's, however, was already drained.

"A final *salud*," and Fernando lifted his glass toward the back pasture. "A final *salud* to my friend, Henry."

"To Henry," someone spoke, breaking the awkward silence, and everyone drained his glass. The sun's last rays were rapidly dipping below the horizon, but the semi-darkness was suddenly brightened as Damon, on cue from Charlotte, turned on the television.

"And now a breaking story from Houston," the T.V. correspondent informed. "We are now speaking to Shannon Crate with the Houston D.A.'s office about the arrest of prominent Houston socialite, Mrs. Emery Burroughs."

The snapshot of a handsome and still beautiful brunette was flashed on the screen.

"I'll be..." Corvel muttered and fixed his eye on the television.

"Mrs. Burroughs came in voluntarily today," Shannon told the interviewer. "She has just signed a confession to the wrongful death of her ex-husband, Henry Sweigurt, who was thought to have been accidently drowned last June just outside of Austin."

"Can you give us any more information?" the reporter probed with unusual courtesy.

"We've been working on the case for several weeks now. The final confirmation came last week, when we contacted Mrs. Burroughs' attorney."

"As you know, Ben," the correspondent said to his Austin anchor, "Just yesterday, our local Houston station reported that Mr. Emery Burroughs, wealthy Houston oil man, filed a Chapter Eleven Bankruptcy Petition. Apparently, the recent slump in oil profits did him in. It appears that his assets were stretched pretty tight, and there is some hint of indictments against him for attempted market manipulation and fraudulent bank loans."

"Our office will be issuing a statement in the morning,' Shannon interrupted, disappointed to have the interviewer cease his questions, and thus volunteering information, something Charlotte guessed he would hear about from the DA. He added, "I'd especially like to thank our clerical staff in Austin, the members of the Emerson branch." And then Shannon quite distinctly winked into the camera.

"Shannon, outrageous as ever," thought Charlotte, and she remembered the Ralph Waldo Emerson quotation she had taught him. It was Shannon's favorite:

"Whoso would be a man must be a nonconformist."

He was certainly that; he was certainly that.

***

"It was her! It was her!" Corvel said as soon as the TV clicked off. "She was the lady I saw with Henry at the Type Store."

"The one whose car you hit," Charlotte added. "That's how we traced her, you know, Corvel. So your rammed pickup and chivalrous civic response paid off."

Thirteen pairs of eyes looked to Charlotte for further enlightenment, which, of course, was how she earned her bread and butter. With methodical patience and clarity she outlined the beginnings of her doubts, starting from the alligator boots and continuing through the forgotten eyeglasses.

"I don't think I would have given it so much thought" - here Charlotte hesitated and looked directly at Fernando - "if it hadn't been for you, Fernando. You really fretted over that note, and your instincts, you know, were right."

She paused and then ventured, "You don't still have it with you, do you?" Fernando withdrew the paper from his wallet and handed it to her. "It certainly is Henry's handwriting. You said that yourself, but what Henry really wrote was,

Gone to Taylor.

Back late.

The 3:00 p.m. was added, and the "L" changed to a clumsy "G." But I'm getting ahead of myself.

"Corvel remembered that Henry is talking 'close and serious' to this classy woman, who left with him some time before noon with Henry looking a little tipsy.

"But he wasn't tipsy at all, and again, Fernando, it was your inner conviction and sincere belief that convinced me that Henry wasn't drunk. And then, quite by chance, I found a newspaper article that said how insulin shock looks like drunkenness."

"The sugar sickness," nodded Fernando.

"Well, here's the rest of what Mrs. Burroughs told the D A - I have it unofficially, though it's pretty much wrapped up by now: She had come here to talk Henry into selling his last 100 acres - you remember that she still had joint ownership. She and her husband were in a pretty tight corner financially, and all the Houston fat cats had the wind up about the new Manor airport and the land prices going up."

"But I read in the paper last week, that the city is cancelling plans or tabling them," Lucille interjected. "Something about a budget shortfall."

"That's exactly right, and I guess it was the final irony that induced Mrs. Burroughs to cash it in and confess. No quick sale and profit could save them now. Anyway," Charlotte continued," she was pretty desperate but didn't admit it to Henry, which was her mistake if you ask me."

"Henry, he would help her if he knows," the trusting Fernando volunteered, and everyone tried to act as though they shared his faith.

"Well, Henry just laughed it off, asking her for a loan from her rich oilman husband, and then he asked her back to the old place for a drink. She went with him in his truck."

"Still the ol' dog I remember," Corvel chuckled.

"Well, whatever his romantic intentions, after the drinks were poured at his place, he started to feel pretty sick. Henry knew he'd better get to his doctor in Taylor - he'd been having trouble with regulating his insulin lately, he told her - and so he wrote the original note to Fernando. I guess faster and simpler than a phone call.

"Mrs. Burroughs drove Henry's pickup as he was pretty groggy by this time, but she didn't know about the bridge work. In the steady downpour, she couldn't see too well and followed the red claw cut to the side and found herself halfway down the ditch before she knew it. With Henry slumped in the cab, she walked up the bank and over the partly completed bridge, at first looking for help, she says."

"She weren't really a bad woman. I remember her when she and Henry was first married," Lucille interrupted. "Kind of sweet and gentle, like a good heifer milk cow, with those big, wide, brown eyes." Her listeners now imagined Mrs. Burroughs with a new insight and nodded sympathetically. "I believe she was looking for help, just like she says," Lucille finished.

"But on the bridge," Charlotte continued, when she looked down on the car with Henry probably unconscious and then saw the creek bed rising...well, she 'succumbed to temptation,' as Mrs. Burroughs herself put it, and merely walked to her car and drove off. That was at precisely 12:30," Charlotte added, proud of her detective work. "Just when *The Flintstones* is on T.V. - in June, that is."

She went on to explain her hunch about children playing in the rain and how young Valerie Schmidt, who had seen the pickup, had watched the woman climb up from the ditch, and saw her walk over the bridge to her car.

"What remained was tracing the license plate numbers that Corvel already had, and checking the background of Mrs. Burroughs. Even I was surprised when Shannon told me how prominent she was, but I was flabbergasted when the Department of Public records listed her as "the once Mrs. Henry Sweigurt." Here she drew a breath and, teacher like, asked if there were any questions.

"What about the note? Why did she add the 3:00 PM and change "Late" to "Gate"? Damon asked.

"Oh, I'd forgotten. Well, the 3:00 time was an alibi, because Mrs. Burroughs was attending a charity ball at 5:00 in Houston--plenty of publicity, witnesses, and photos to verify her attendance. If Henry were definitely alive at 3:00, that cleared her, because the drive to Houston was almost three hours. As it was, even by leaving Henry at 12:30, she was hard pressed to make it on time to the ball, what with all the bad weather and such..."

An eye from Damon steered her back to his second question.

"And the "gate," a suggestion from Henry, sort of. It seems his last somewhat incoherent thoughts were of his stranded cattle and the back gate in Taylor that he hoped Fernando had opened."

With this she smiled at Fernando, who drew himself to his full five feet, and nodded reproachfully at the others. Then, turning dramatically, with the easy grace of a bullfighter, he raised his glass a second time to the back pasture.

"Salud, my friend. *Salud."*

Recipes from Oktoberfest

Recipe courtesy of Gary.

GARY CHOIRBY: Charlotte's professor husband, whose skeptical mind balances his wife's impetuous one. A naturally quiet scholar, when he speaks up Charlotte knows it's important.

Grilled Sausages

Sausage should always be heated to an internal temperature of 165°F. When the natural juices of the sausage break through the casing, that's a great indicator that the sausage is ready.

Always grill sausage over indirect heat. Simply build your coals on one side of the grill and place the sausage on the other side of the grill. If using a gas grill, cook the sausage on the opposite end from the heat. Grill at 300-350°F turning the sausage once during cooking time. Fully Smoked sausage should be grilled for 15-20 minutes until 165°F. Fresh (Raw) sausage should be grilled for 40-50 minutes until 165°F. The heat can be reduced as desired, but in this case the cooking time will need to be increased. Southside Market.com

Recipe courtesy of Gary

GARY CHOIRBY: Charlotte's professor husband, whose skeptical mind balances his wife's impetuous one. A naturally quiet scholar, when he speaks up Charlotte knows it's important.

Foil-Wrapped Corn on the Cob

<u>**Directions for Grilled Corn:**</u>

<u>**Two Seasoning Recipes for Grilled Corn on the Cob:**</u>

<u>**Cilantro and Lime**</u> (a yummy grilled seasoned corn on the cob recipe with a little lime juice for added flavor.

On each piece of corn, spread 1-2 Tablespoons of butter onto it. Now you can sprinkle it with Parmesan cheese or add a little minced fresh cilantro (my favorite!). Squeeze a tiny bit of lime on top.

Garlic and Thyme (Another yummy one!)
Mix butter, garlic, thyme salt, and pepper together in a small bowl. Rub about 1 Tablespoon of the mixture on each ear of the corn. Sprinkle with a little Parmesan & parsley.

Directions
Take your corn and pull back the husks and peel the entire husk off. Some people like leaving the

husks on to grill the corn in the husks, but I'd rather take them off.

Remove the silk from it. (This is a great activity for your kids. Our kids actually ask me if they can 'peel the corn' for me, so I send them onto the porch with corn, a large bowl, and a garbage can.)

Rinse it well with the cold water.

You can either leave them big or cut each piece in half.

Season with one of the seasoning recipes found above. You can even leave it plain and just season it with a little butter, salt & black pepper. One of my friends even likes to season it with cayenne pepper.

Now wrap the corn (each piece individually) in aluminum foil.

Grill the corn for 15 to 20 minutes (you will want to place them in high heat - around 350-400 degrees)

Optional: *You can take it off, unwrap it and place the corn back on (without the foil) for a minute longer, to let it get the grill marks.*

Serve it immediately. This is always a family favorite!
Your Modern Family.com

Recipe courtesy of Charlotte

CHARLOTTE CHOIRBY: Quirky English teacher who suspects foul play in Henry's death near the old ranch house that she and her family are renovating.

Spicy Bacon Baked Beans

Creamy, salty perfect baked beans!

Ingredients

- 2 28 oz. can pork & beans
- 1 lb. bacon cut and fried
- 1 onion chopped small
- 1/4 cup brown sugar
- 1 tsp. ground mustard
- 1 8 oz. can tomato sauce
- 1 jalapeno diced
-

Instructions

1. In fry pan start browning cut bacon. When bacon is almost brown add onion and jalapeño and sauté until onions are translucent and jalapeños are soft.
2. Drain excess grease from pan.
3. Stir all ingredients together.
4. Bake at 350 for 1-1.5 hours

-Des and Kadee

Oh So Delicioso.com

https://ohsodelicioso.com/baked-beans/

Recipe courtesy of Charlotte

CHARLOTTE CHOIRBY: Quirky English teacher who suspects foul play in Henry's death near the old ranch house she and her family are renovating.

Mustang Grape Dry Red Wine (Chateau de Charlotte)

Mustang Grapes (Vitis mustangensis) are native to the southern United States and grow wild throughout Texas. If you pluck one off the vine and have a taste, you'll be in for a shock. These grapes have very high acidity and a harsh bitterness. They taste terrible, and the acidity is so high it can even irritate your skin or mouth.

However, our recipe makes a delicious wine and shows how to reduce the acidity. And while Mustang Wine is often too sweet, our recipe makes a **dry red wine.**

Ingredients

6 lbs. black Mustang Grapes

- 1-1/2 lbs. granulated sugar
- 6 pints water
- 1 crushed Campden tablet
- wine yeast and nutrient

Directions
Remove the stems and wash the grapes. While wearing rubber gloves, crush the grapes in a crock or polyethylene pail.

Add all ingredients except yeast. Stir well and cover for 24 hours, then add yeast.

The must will form a floating "cap" of skins and seeds which should be pushed under and stirred twice daily for 5 to 7 days. Strain and press pulp well to extract liquid.

Measure acidity, then follow one of the *methods below to reduce the acidity to 7 parts per thousand (p.p.t.) tartaric if necessary.

Pour into secondary fermentation vessel, fit airlock, and let stand three weeks.

Rack and top up, then rack again in three months and add fining. Bottle ten days after fining. May taste immediately, but improves remarkably with age (3-4 years). [Adapted from a traditional "wild grape" recipe.]

***Reducing Acidity**
If the acidity of the grapes is too high, further acid reduction may be required. Here are three methods....
Acid Reduction with Calcium Carbonate: *For liquors with acid levels of 10 p.p.t. or more, calcium carbonate is traditionally used to reduce*

acid through precipitation. A measured 2.5 grams of calcium carbonate will reduce the acidity of one gallon of wine or liquor by one p.p.t. For best results, split the liquor into two equal portions and add the calcium carbonate to one while stirring vigorously. Carbon dioxide will be given off and cause foaming. Chill the treated liquor several days and then siphon it off the lees of calcium carbonate into the untreated portion. The addition of a teaspoon of yeast energizer may be required to reactivate fermentation after treatment.

Acid Reduction with Potassium Bicarbonate: *For liquors with acid levels of 8 to 10 p.p.t., potassium bicarbonate treatment can be used to reduce acid through precipitation and neutralization. A measured 3.4 grams or 0.1 oz. of potassium bicarbonate will reduce the acidity of one gallon of wine or liquor by one p.p.t. The compound is stirred directly into the full batch, then chilled to facilitate precipitation of potassium bicarbonate lees. The addition of a teaspoon of yeast energizer may be required to reactivate fermentation after treatment.*

Acid Reduction through Water Dilution: *This is the least desirable method, only because the Mustang Grape flavor is diluted and the resulting wine will suffer. The acid is inversely proportional to the volume of liquor, so the steps in reducing acidity from 10 p.p.t., for example, to 7 p.p.t., are: (1) 7 / 10 = 0.70 (2) 100*

/ 0.70 = 1.428 (3) 1.428 x 128 (oz. per gallon) = 182.784 total oz. required (4) 182.784 (total required) - 128 (oz. per gallon) = 54.784 (oz. per gallon required to be added).

Winemaking jackkeller.net

Recipe courtesy of Lucille

LUCILLE: Charlotte's feisty and shrewd ranch neighbor. A fountain of homespun wisdom on dewberry picking and avoiding diamondbacks in the process, she can talk without missing a beat, even with a Camel cigarette tucked under her up side lip.

Rustic Rosemary Bread

Ingredients

- 1 1/2 tsp. active dry yeast
- 1 cup warm water, 110-115F
- 2 tsp. white sugar
- 2 tsp. fine salt
- 3 TB extra virgin olive oil
- 2 1/2 cups bread flour
- 1 TB dried rosemary
- 1/4 tsp. freshly ground black pepper
- 1/2 tsp. dried oregano
- 1 head of roasted garlic
- extra olive oil for brushing on top and serving
- coarse sea salt for sprinkling on top
- balsamic vinegar for serving
- clean water in spray bottle

Directions

1. In large bowl, Sprinkle yeast into 1 cup warm water. Mix in the sugar and salt. Let sit for

about 10 minutes or until it foams. Add in olive oil. Add flour and knead (by hand or stand mixer) for about 10 minutes. Add rosemary, black pepper, and oregano. Knead another 5 minutes. Finally, gently knead in roasted garlic by hand, about 1 minute. Dough should come together well at this point; slightly sticky is fine.

2. Place dough ball in well-oiled bowl, turning dough a few times so that dough surfaces are protected by oil. Tightly cover bowl with cling wrap. Place in warm, draft-free area to rise until dough is doubled, approx. 1 hour, depending on room temp (if your room is cooler, it could take 2 hours.)

3. After dough is doubled, punch it down and shape into a rounded loaf. Using sharp knife, make a crisscross design on top. Place rounded loaf on greased baking sheet. Cover up loaf with large mixing bowl inverted over it. Make sure bowl is large enough that it gives your loaf room to rise. Let rise until doubled again, approx. 1 hour.

4. After dough has doubled again, gently brush with olive oil, sprinkle with coarse sea salt and a bit more rosemary. Bake at 375F for 25-30 minutes, spraying loaf with water once during the middle of baking. Bump oven up to 425F and spray loaf with water again. Watch carefully - bake just until top is a nice golden brown, taking care not to over bake.

5. Serve bread fresh and warm, with your favorite blend of good olive oil, freshly ground black pepper, and balsamic vinegar!
Chew Out Loud.com

Recipe courtesy of Zabrina, wife of

TYRONE CARTWRIGHT: "Henry's pup," his half-black out-of-wedlock son. A fine man, blacksmith, and beekeeper, he rids Charlotte and Gary of a huge hive inside their ranch house walls.

Deep Fried Biscuits with Honey Butter

Also great for breakfast!

Ingredients

For the biscuits

- 1 tube refrigerated biscuits any style
- Oil for frying
-

For the honey butter

- 1/4 pound butter
- 1 tablespoon honey
- 1/8 teaspoon ground cinnamon
- 1/8 teaspoon vanilla extract

Instructions

- Heat oil in a deep fryer or Dutch oven (you'll need 2"-3" worth) to 375 F.
- Open biscuits and separate. Use your hands to stretch them out slightly, forming little discs.
- Working in batches, fry biscuits 2-3 minutes per

side until golden brown. Remove to a paper towel-lined plate.

▪

For the honey butter

▪ Melt butter in a small sauté pan over low heat.

▪ Add honey, cinnamon and vanilla. Stir. Keep warm until ready to use.

-Mike Life's aTomato.com

http://www.lifesatomato.com/2015/03/11/deep-fried-biscuits-honey-butter/

Recipe courtesy of

FERNANDO MUNOZ: Perhaps the only person who actually did like Henry, his partner in some cattle they kept in nearby Taylor. Fernando is the first beside Charlotte to think Henry's death suspicious.

Homemade Tamales

"I had been looking for a Tamale recipe for years. One day I went to the international market and stood in the Mexican aisle till a woman with a full cart came by. I just asked her if she knew how to make Tamales. This is her recipe with a few additions from me. The pork can be substituted with either chicken or beef. This is great served with refried beans and a salad." - Saddieca

Ingredients

Tamale Filling:
1 1/4 pounds pork loin
1 large onion, halved
1 clove garlic
4 dried California chile pods
2 cups water
1 1/2 teaspoons salt

Tamale Dough:
2 cups masa harina
1 (10.5 ounce) can beef broth
1 teaspoon baking powder
1/2 teaspoon salt
2/3 cup lard

1 (8 ounce) package dried corn husks
1 cup sour cream

Directions
Place pork into a Dutch oven with onion and garlic, and add water to cover. Bring to a boil, then reduce heat to low and simmer until the meat is cooked through, about 2 hours.

Use rubber gloves to remove stems and seeds from the chile pods. Place chiles in a saucepan with 2 cups of water. Simmer, uncovered, for 20 minutes, then remove from heat to cool.

Transfer the chiles and water to a blender and blend until smooth. Strain the mixture, stir in salt, and set aside. Shred the cooked meat and mix in one cup of the chile sauce.

Soak the corn husks in a bowl of warm water. In a large bowl, beat the lard with a tablespoon of the broth until fluffy. Combine the masa harina, baking powder and salt; stir into the lard mixture, adding more broth as necessary to form a spongy dough.

Spread the dough out over the corn husks to 1/4 to 1/2 inch thickness. Place one tablespoon of the meat filling into the center. Fold the sides of the husks in toward the center and place in a steamer.

Steam for 1 hour.

Remove tamales from husks and drizzle remaining chile sauce over. Top with sour cream. For a creamy sauce, mix sour cream into the chile sauce.
All Recipes.com

Recipe courtesy of

CHRIS CAVECROFT: Owner of the patch of land next to Charlotte's, he shares a disputed fence line and pond with Henry, who was about to sue him over it before his demise. With Henry gone, that worry disappears.

Warn Red-Skinned German Potato Salad

A nice change of pace from our American mayonnaise based potato salad. Apple cider vinegar and warm bacon grease form the delicious dressing. (Different Drummer prefers hers without the sugar, but you decide.)

Ingredients

- 2 pounds red potatoes
- 1 teaspoon salt, for boiling the potatoes
- 12 ounces bacon
- 1/3 cup apple cider vinegar
- 3 tablespoons sugar (Optional)
- 3 Tablespoons sour cream
- 1 tablespoon Dijon mustard
- 1/2 teaspoon salt
- Freshly ground black pepper
- 1 tablespoon minced fresh garlic, about 3 large cloves
- 1/2 cup chopped fresh parsley

Instructions

1. Scrub the potatoes and cut any large potatoes in half so that all of the potatoes are approximately equally sized. Place the potatoes in a large pot and cover with cold water. Bring to a boil and stir in 1 teaspoon of salt. Reduce heat and simmer the potatoes for 15 to 20 minutes or until tender when stabbed with a fork. Drain the water. Leaving the potatoes in the pot, return the pot to the still-hot (but turned off) burner. Leave the lid off of the pot and allow the potatoes to steam dry for a couple minutes.

2. Set another large pot over medium heat and, using kitchen shears, cut the bacon strips into approximately 1-inch pieces directly into the pot. Cook the bacon, stirring occasionally, until crispy. While the bacon is cooking, cut the potatoes into 1/2-inch thick slices, cutting any extremely large slices in half. Set aside. Once the bacon is done, remove the pot from the stove and use a slotted spoon to remove the bacon pieces to a plate or bowl while leaving the bacon grease in the pot (I had about 1/4 cup).

3. Slowly and carefully add vinegar, sugar, sour cream, Dijon, salt, and pepper to the pot of bacon grease. Place the pot back on the burner, bring the mixture to a simmer, and stir for a couple of minutes. Stir the minced garlic into the mixture and cook for 30 seconds to 1 minute, until the garlic starts to turn a light golden. Remove the pot from the heat and toss in the

sliced potatoes, gently mixing until potatoes have absorbed all of the liquid. Carefully fold in the cooked bacon pieces and chopped parsley. Transfer the potato salad to a serving dish and serve hot or warm. Potato salad should not sit at room temperature for more than two hours before refrigerating any leftovers.

*Notes
Make sure that the pot is off of the burner and the bacon grease has slightly cooled before slowly and carefully adding the vinegar (in order to prevent the mixture from potentially bubbling up)
-Samantha at Five Heart Home. Com

Recipe courtesy of Sue Cavecroft, wife of

CHRIS CAVECROFT: Owner of the patch of land next to Charlotte's, he shares a disputed fence line and pond with Henry, who was about to sue him over it before his demise. With Henry gone, that worry disappears.

Aunt June's Refrigerator Pickles

"Here is the recipe that I got from my Aunt June, who was a farmer's wife in south central Minnesota. The recipe is a great way to enjoy all those cucumbers that appear in August." (Or right now if you live a bit further south.) - Judy Reisner

- 3 cups apple cider vinegar
- 3 cups sugar
- 1/3 cup salt
- 1 tsp. celery salt
- 1 tsp. mustard seeds
- 1/2 tsp. turmeric

Sliced onion (1 large or several small as desired)
Peeled and sliced cucs (ten to twelve depending on the size)

2 quart jar or 2 one quart jars.

Warm the first six ingredients to dissolve the sugar and release the flavor of the spices. Pack the jar with cucumbers and onion mix and pour the liquid into the jars. Keep refrigerated. They are ready to enjoy in a few hours. As they get used up you can add additional cucumbers to the brine for more pickles.

Recipe courtesy of

ELROY: A semi-retired carpenter, a whiz at water witching and killing diamondbacks with a single hammer like blow.

Dutch Apple Pie

Ingredients

Crust
1 cup Gold Medal™ all-purpose flour
1½ teaspoons salt
1/3cup plus 1 tablespoon shortening
2 to 3 tablespoons cold water

Filling
8 cups sliced cored peeled apples
½ cup granulated sugar
¼ cup Gold Medal™ all-purpose flour
¼ teaspoon ground cinnamon
1 tablespoon lemon juice

Topping
½ cup unsalted butter, softened
1 cup Gold Medal™ all-purpose flour
2/3 cup packed brown sugar
t1 Tablespoon granulated sugar

Directions
In medium bowl, mix 1 cup flour and the salt. Cut in shortening, using pastry blender (or pulling 2 table knives through ingredients in

opposite directions), until particles are size of small peas. Sprinkle with cold water, 1 tablespoon at a time, tossing with fork until all flour is moistened and pastry almost leaves side of bowl (1 to 2 teaspoons more water can be added if necessary). Gather pastry into a ball. Shape into flattened round on lightly floured surface. Wrap flattened round of pastry in plastic wrap, and refrigerate about 45 minutes or until dough is firm and cold, yet pliable. This allows the shortening to become slightly firm, which helps make the baked pastry more flaky. If refrigerated longer, let pastry soften slightly before rolling.

Heat oven to 400°F. On surface sprinkled with flour, using floured rolling pin, roll pastry dough into circle 2 inches larger than 9-inch pie plate. Fold pastry into fourths; place in pie plate. Unfold and ease into plate, pressing firmly against bottom and side and being careful not to stretch pastry, which will cause it to shrink when baked. Trim overhanging edge of pastry 1 inch from rim of pie plate. Fold and roll pastry under, even with plate; flute as desired.

In large bowl, toss Filling ingredients. Pour into pie plate, mounding apples toward center.

In medium bowl, use pastry blender or fingers to mix butter, 1 cup flour and the brown sugar until a crumb forms. Sprinkle evenly over top of pie. Sprinkle 1 tablespoon granulated sugar on top.

Bake 45 to 55 minutes or until pie crust and crumb topping are deep golden brown and filling begins to bubble. Transfer to cooling rack to cool.

-Stephanie Wise: Betty Crocker.com

Kathy Borich

CPSIA information can be obtained
at www.ICGtesting.com
Printed in the USA
LVHW032225110122
708278LV00007B/323

9 781638 680338